"I've kept my side of the bargain!"

"Bargain?" he teased. "What bargain was this?"

"The bargain that if I humored you you'd go away?" Ana reminded him sweetly. "So I take it you're leaving in the morning?"

"I said no deal." Jed grinned. Unrepentantly, he raked a thoughtful hand through his hair. "I've no intention of going anywhere...."

Ana glared at him, eyes wider. "You're planning on staying all week?"

"I'm touched by your enthusiasm."

ROSALIE
ASH

Dangerous Nights

Harlequin Books

TORONTO • NEW YORK • LONDON
AMSTERDAM • PARIS • SYDNEY • HAMBURG
STOCKHOLM • ATHENS • TOKYO • MILAN
MADRID • WARSAW • BUDAPEST • AUCKLAND

ISBN 0-373-18652-5

DANGEROUS NIGHTS

First North American Publication 1997.

CHAPTER ONE

'ANA?' The deep, male greeting came from the shadows by the stage door. Halting abruptly in her stride, long blonde hair flying behind her in her haste, she swivelled to scan the darkness.

'Anastasia French?' The owner of the voice stepped towards her. He was silhouetted now against the light from the doorway. She could make out only a tall, tough-looking man in denims and brown leather flying jacket. A black baseball cap was pulled well forward over his eyes. He was holding a theatre programme in his hands. An autograph hunter. She hugged her coat around her, glanced warily at his shadowed face. In her old velvet jacket, her floppy black velvet hat covering most of her hair, she was rarely spotted by one of the audience. She wasn't one of the well-known members of this season's Royal Shakespeare Company. Not by any stretch of the imagination.

But there was something familiar about *him*. His build, height and, above all, his voice. Her heart flipped annoyingly in her chest.

'Hi, did you enjoy the play?' She smiled politely, waiting for the request to sign the programme. A group of fellow actors brushed past her. She exchanged goodnights with them as they went.

'I didn't watch the play,' the man murmured coolly. 'I was intrigued to see if the Anastasia French in the programme was the Ana French I knew, a few years back.'

This time the jolt in her heart felt more like a miniature earthquake. Whatever the last few years had taught her about disguising her emotions, she had difficulty clamping down the surge of reaction. Mixed up with anger, pride, apprehension were a host of other emotions, less easily identified...

'Jed?' Her voice was usually husky, rich and quite deep. She hardly recognised the breathless squeak which came out now.

He pushed the baseball cap back, then flipped it off. He had brown hair, worn longish, tousled back into crisp, thick layers which brushed the collar of his jacket. A hard, unconventionally attractive face. Long, narrowed, grey-green eyes. An unreadable gaze, which was achingly familiar...

'Hello, Ana.'

'What are you doing here?' she managed. Her pulse-rate was still galloping at a hundred miles an hour. It didn't make sense still, to feel such an intense reaction, after all this time. She'd got over Jed Steele ages ago. Hadn't she? He'd been her baptism of fire. The big mistake all teenagers had to make before they grew up, grew their protective layer, grew accustomed to the cruel old world around them.

'Hoping to get this programme signed?' He shot her a cool, brief grin, holding open the page where the cast list was printed. 'It says in here you're understudying a major role. Congratulations. That's a big career move, isn't it?'

'If I get to do it, which is by no means guaranteed.' She spoke as evenly as she could, scrawling her name with an unsteady hand. 'There. Happy? I wish I could say it was *nice* to see you again, Jed...'

Now why had she said that? Showing bitterness, giving herself away, after all this time?

He caught her arm as she began to swing away. She turned her head, stiffening at his touch. His eyes were intent, searching her face. That look made her heart sink.

'I don't see you for four years,' he queried lazily, 'and all I get is a twenty-second conversation?'

'What did you have in mind?' Her defensiveness was amusing him, she realised bitterly. His hold on her arm, even through the thickness of her coat, was making the surface of her skin contract into tiny shivers of awareness.

But how could she fail to be aware of him? Jed wasn't the kind of man you could ignore. Tall, arrogant, faintly menacing, he radiated strength, cynicism and forceful virility in almost equal measures. How he managed to restrain them into his cool, watchful manner, a hallmark of his character, she'd never worked out. But then, when it came to what made Jed Steele the way he was, she'd never succeeded in working anything out...

'How about a drink?' Jed was suggesting, in that deep voice which had always made her stomach melt. 'In the pub up the road?' The invitation was casual, but already he was falling into stride beside her, one hand still on her upper arm. The proprietorial air was unnerving.

'I'm much too tired for that...'

'Just one drink. Then I'll walk you home.'

Walk her *home*? Who did he think he was? Turning up after a four-year silence, after the cruel fiasco of their last meeting, and calmly taking over. Anger surged, but she controlled it. The more she protested, a small voice reminded her, the more she gave herself away. Fake indifference. Feign uninterest. With a massive effort, she shrugged lightly.

'OK. I suppose one drink won't hurt.' A yawn behind her hand gave credence to the performance. If he felt affronted, he gave no sign. But he'd always been infuriatingly...deadpan. She might have chosen acting as her profession, but Jed's talent for masking his thoughts would win him an Oscar.

With a glass of white wine in front of her, she met that hard, narrowed gaze over the corner table in the smoky bar, and remembered precisely, in painful detail, why she'd once felt that instant, devastating attraction...

'You look well, Ana.'

The simple words were no more than a polite formality. She was imagining any husky quality in his voice, wasn't she? Fooling herself that those cold eyes held a hidden gleam in their depths?

Taking a shaky breath, she silently lectured herself to be very, very careful. It would be fatal to read anything into this surprise meeting.

'Thank you. So do you. So... what are you doing in Stratford?' she managed stiffly. 'Apart from hanging around the stage door holding programmes for plays you haven't seen.'

Under the lazy, non-committal regard she had to summon all her poise to flip off the velvet hat idly, rake long fingers casually through her thick blonde hair. But she met his light green eyes with a calm brown gaze.

Some of the cast from tonight's play in the main theatre were gathered around the bar. Curious glances were being angled in their direction. Out of the corner of her eye, she could see Camilla and Pru respecting her privacy, but covertly noting Jed's lean brand of sex appeal. Theatre gossip being what it was, her unknown companion would be the subject of delighted conjecture and discussion for at least three days.

'Just passing through.' The detached scrutiny was calmly raking her from head to toe. Where his eyes moved, she felt a shiver of physical response. Could he see the effect he had on her? She gripped her hands together in her lap, agonisingly conscious of his power over her. Beneath her loose, scoop-necked white sweatshirt, she was braless. Her small, high breasts had tightened involuntarily under that calculating appraisal...

'So what's new?' She fortified her nerves with a sip of wine, appalled at the way her hand shook. 'You spend your life "just passing through", don't you?'

'No worse surely than spending your life pretending to be someone else?' There was a dangerous gleam in Jed's eyes.

Despite her determination to fight her feelings, she found herself staring at his face, wide-eyed, almost mesmerised. She was trapped then, in that poker-player's gaze. Jed had always possessed the knack of concentrating visually, unblinking, apparently indefinitely, without moving a muscle.

'If that's your definition of the acting profession, it just shows your miserable lack of culture,' she managed at last, dropping her eyes. 'So how long does "just passing through" mean this time? One night? One week?'

'I'm not sure yet.'

He took a mouthful of his drink. He hadn't switched his tastes in that area, she noticed, with a stab of resentment. Still iced mineral water with a wedge of lemon. Maybe he felt the need to be on red alert every waking moment of the day?

Alcohol might blur that robot-style control of his...

He flexed broad shoulders, rested one booted foot on the rung of the stool beside him. Under the soft leather jacket, he wore a black polo-necked jumper. It looked like cashmere. The fine wool faithfully emphasised the rock-hard contour of his chest, the ridged flatness of diaphragm and solar plexus. His body resembled his personality, she reflected uneasily. Hard and controlled. Constantly on guard. It was disturbing, she reflected, how much she remembered about him. More than disturbing. Terrifying...

'So how are things?' He followed up his non-committal reply with a soft query. 'Are you enjoying being in Stratford?'

'What do you think?' Her caution slipped a little. 'It's brilliant. I wake up every day and think, I'm so incredibly lucky! Being with the Royal Shakespeare Company is something I always dreamed of doing. Never quite believed possible.'

'You're good. I've seen you do Shakespeare, remember?' He dismissed her modesty with deadpan insensitivity. 'I could have told you four years ago that you'd make it, Ana.'

Surely he couldn't be referring to that humiliating episode in the garden, at Farthingley? The memory brought heat to her face. She couldn't think of the last time she'd blushed... at least, yes, she could. It had been that weekend, at

Farthingley. That forty-eight hours in her life when all her novice feelings and emotions had seemed to spring to the surface of her skin and glow like phosphorus...

But now here she was, confident Anastasia French, twenty-three years old, rising young star, currently appearing on one of the most famous stages in the world, blushing again, like a schoolgirl on her first date—she could hate him for that alone...

Catching Camilla's eye, she dragged herself together. Was she as lobster-red as she felt?

'What are you doing these days?' she countered quickly. 'Or is that still classified information?'

The grey-green eyes cooled.

'I scrape along.'

Anastasia stared at him for a long moment. Then she slowly shook her head. 'You "scrape along"?' she echoed. She was quite unable to hide her angry frustration. 'I've never met anyone like you, Jed Steele! You're so... *barricaded*! You—you lead your life in total secrecy! That day I first met you, you were "scraping along" at my father's house, doing some unspecified, totally mysterious job for him during that conference weekend. Most men I've met, *normal* men, admit to being... actors, or theatre directors, or... or musicians, or even businessmen, accountants, firemen, plumbers...'

'Spare me your sordid memoirs, Ana.' His eyes gleamed with rare humour.

Her jaw dropped. After a moment's strangled silence, she said frostily, 'I was giving *hypothetical* examples, not listing my sexual encounters!'

'I believe you.'

She took a long breath. 'Where have you been working recently?'

'Abroad.'

'Where abroad?'

'Washington. Paris. Brussels. Geneva.' A heavy gold watch glinted at his wrist as he reached for his glass. She stared at the lean shape of his hand, the long, well-shaped fingers, the flexible ripple of tendons under the duskily tanned skin. A sprinkle of dark hair roughened the back of his hand, disappeared up the strong wrist under the black cashmere. Wrenching her eyes away with an effort, dismayed at his power to mesmerise her like this, she cast around for a flippant retort.

'I've got it. You're an international jewel thief,' she said decisively. 'That's how you get to drive black Porsches and own huge town houses in half a dozen different cities all over the world...'

'How do you know what kind of houses I own?'

'Something my father said, I expect. But don't worry,' she added with an edge of sarcasm, 'he didn't divulge anything else about you! Your guilty secrets are safe!'

Jed's gaze was wryly non-committal. He watched as she impatiently drained her glass. 'Would you like another wine?'

'No. I'm going to head for bed...'

'I'll walk you home.'

'There's no need to bother. My digs are only just round the corner...'

'It's no bother.' He stood up, reached for her jacket and held it out for her.

'How *gentlemanly*.' She couldn't resist the acerbic tease, although she was trembling inside as she slid her arms in. 'I'd have thought you were better at helping girls *off* with their clothes.'

'That's pretty childish, Anastasia. Don't forget your hat.'

Flustered, she turned and snatched up the velvet hat, pulled it on hard, waved quickly to her friends, and escaped into the night air. Thank goodness it was so cold. Her cheeks felt as if they were on fire...

September was nearly over. An early frost had sharpened the air. The heady scent of petunias and nicotiana had been almost obliterated.

'Why did you come to see me at the stage door tonight?' she demanded as he began to walk with her. He had an easy, prowling way of walking. It reminded her of a very large panther, shadowing silently beside her.

'Just...to say hello,' he countered calmly. 'Renew acquaintance.'

'Why would you want to do that?' She shivered as she glared up at his dark profile.

'Does there have to be a particular reason?' He sounded coolly preoccupied, almost cagey. 'Is this the way you normally walk home? Alone?'

'You are such a—a cold-blooded *bastard*!' she burst out involuntarily. She stopped to cross the road quickly, conscious only of the urge to get away from him.

'Anastasia——'

Whatever he'd been about to say was abruptly cut short. A car had turned the corner and was roaring along the road towards them. With a speed which took her breath away and left her mentally reeling, she found herself half lifted, half pushed to the far pavement, and then pinned against the low stone wall enclosing the river gardens.

The car shot blindly past. The engine noise faded. It disappeared. Shaking all over, she struggled to free herself from Jed's vice-like hold.

'Are you all right?'

'Yes,' she said crossly. 'Of course I'm all right. For goodness' sake, I'm not stupid—I saw the car...'

'He didn't seem to have seen you,' Jed said drily, releasing her, and dusting her down with an unreadable gleam in his eyes. 'You're trembling. Are you prone to near accidents like that, Anastasia?'

'No! And I'm quite capable of looking after myself! But...thanks anyway.' It took an effort to say it. He was right, the near miss seemed to have shaken her up more than she'd realised.

'No problem. Do you usually cut through these gardens late at night?'

'Yes. Normally I...I walk with a friend from the theatre. And Stratford is really quite a nice little town, you know. It has very few muggers and perverts lurking in the bushes...'

'No town is free of those.'

'Well, maybe I'm not familiar with whatever sordid world you inhabit.'

'No,' he agreed, 'maybe you're not.'

They'd reached the terraced house she shared with three other members of the company. Searching for her key in her shoulder-bag, she paused uncertainly. Jed showed no signs of bidding her a polite goodnight and vanishing. His deadpan presence at her side implied a definite expectation of being invited in.

'I suppose I *should* be polite and ask you in for—for coffee,' she said shortly, 'but it's late and I'm tired, so...'

As she pushed the key into the lock, the door swung open, unlocked. One of the others must have left in on the latch, for some reason, earlier on. The telephone was ringing.

'Excuse me...' Darting inside, she picked up the receiver. The caller rang off. Replacing the phone on its hook, she was just glaring at it in frustration, when she realised that Jed had followed her inside. Her heart began to thud painfully in her chest. He looked unnervingly large and intimidating in the narrow hall.

'Jed, I'm sorry...I really have to get to bed.'

'Yeah, I know. I'm just curious about where you live.' He spoke with easy confidence, 'Who was that on the phone?'

'No one. They rang off as I answered...'

'Do you share this house with someone else?'

'Three others. They're either all out, or all asleep.'

'Who left the door unlocked?'

Didn't the wretched man miss *anything*?

'I haven't a clue. And right now I couldn't care less!'

'I'll see you up to your room.' There was an air of bleak authority about him suddenly.

She stared at him in mounting bewilderment. What kind of insidious game was he playing, knowing how she must feel about the past? Turning up tonight out of the blue. Following her home. Barging in, uninvited...

'Look, I don't know what you want,' she began hotly, 'but frankly I'd like you to go away and leave me alone, Jed——'

'Ana——'

'Just get *out*...!'

She trailed off abruptly as he took a step closer. He grabbed her shoulders, then hesitated, uncharacteristically. His fingers dug into her, hard and powerful, through the velvet jacket. He had an air of silently calculating the situation. Then, with a soft, four-letter expletive, he slowly closed the gap between then and lowered his head, as if to kiss her.

Ana caught her breath. She couldn't breathe at all. But he didn't kiss her. Maybe her fierce intake of breath had made him think twice? He stopped, within an inch of her mouth, then lifted his head again, his eyes dark with an emotion she didn't recognise.

The shock of his nearness stunned her into terrified confusion—the clean, male smell of him, the remembered shape and feel of his body, a scant half inch from hers, so overpoweringly large, and male, and close. She could remember how it had felt to be moulded with brazen intimacy all the way down, every inch of their contrasting sexuality fused into one... It triggered a wild response. The response was unexpected in its intensity, and yet only too familiar. Humiliatingly familiar. The way he held her, that crucial few millimetres apart from him, had a fierce constraint which transmitted itself to her. There was a subtle hint of violence. As if he was suppressing a potentially dangerous depth of feeling.

He released her. The green eyes were a shade darker. Her heart seemed to expand and swell in her ribcage, her stomach was contorted with anger and fear and, to her eternal humiliation, a contrary and unwelcome shiver of pleasure. 'This is not playing *fair* . . . !'

'Back to games again, Ana? But I'm not playing at all,' he assured her. The thick rasp made every tiny hair prickle on her body. 'Let's go upstairs.' He sounded grimly angry. With her? Or with himself? But why should *he* be angry?

'Go *upstairs*? Look, are you crazy? You expect to be asked to . . . to sleep the *night* here or something? With me? Just . . . just to finish off whatever was left in the air four years ago?'

'You're over-reacting. As usual. I said I'd see you up to your room.' The put-down was coldly ruthless.

Hot and furious, shuddering with emotion, she glared up at him. The notion of physically attacking him was tempting, but swiftly dismissed. No amount of kicks and punches would dent that six-foot wall of masculine arrogance . . .

Turning stiffly on her heel, she marched up the staircase towards her bedroom. Her legs felt like rubber. Flinging open her door, she snapped on the light and made a dramatic gesture with her arms.

'*Voilà!*' she announced icily. 'My bedroom. Satisfied?'

Jed strolled in, and looked bleakly around. The terraced house was early Edwardian, and the high-ceilinged, deep-corniced room was spacious,

with cream walls and a green patterned carpet.
His cool gaze took in the brass and wrought-iron
bed, the rumpled crimson duvet, the battered old
one-legged teddy-bear sprawled on the pillow, the
posters of Hollywood greats plastered on the
walls, the shelves of books, the pile of clothes on
the armchair by the window.

'Tidiness was never your strong point, I recall,'
he murmured, unforgivably.

'If the only reason you've barged your way up
here is to criticise my tidiness ... !' With a degree
of defiance she dragged off her jacket and hat
and threw them to land on top of the clothes pile.
She stood, breathing rather raggedly, a petite,
willowy figure in the floppy white sweatshirt and
black leggings.

Jed ignored her. He'd crossed to the window,
twitched back the heavy red velvet curtains. Impatiently, she marched over to stand beside him.

'It overlooks the church,' she pointed out unnecessarily, suppressing her temper with difficulty. 'Jed, will you please *go*?'

There was a long silence. She couldn't read his
eyes. She couldn't tune in to his thoughts. She'd
never felt more at sea, more bewildered, in her
life.

'Do you want me to go?' The question was
softly abrupt. The steady gaze had locked with
hers. When he let his eyes slide smoothly to the
rapid rise and fall of her breasts, the nipples
visible as tight little points through the soft fabric

of her top, a deep, disturbing confusion began rippling, like invisible waves, right through her.

'What sort of question is that supposed to be?' she shot at him angrily. 'I don't believe this! I should admire your nerve, I suppose. Do you honestly think that because I was . . . *panting* for you to take my virginity four years ago you can just stroll back into my life and haul me into bed with you? After one glass of white wine and half an hour of your famous *non*-conversation?'

'Maybe we don't always know what we want,' he hazarded quietly.

The blatant arrogance took her breath away. 'Oh, no!' she breathed furiously. 'You're the one who didn't know what he wanted, as I recall——!'

A door slammed. Voices on the stairs heralded the return of the others. The tension between Jed and herself was so taut, she felt herself sag with relief.

'Ana? Ana? Are you back?' her friend's voice called along the landing, footsteps coming closer. 'Who was that *dishy* male you were with in the pub . . . ?' Camilla froze on the threshold of the bedroom, and had the grace to look slightly embarrassed.

Exchanging an agitated glance with Jed, Ana gestured weakly at her uninvited guest.

'This is Jed Steele. An old . . . acquaintance. Jed, this is Camilla Browning, one of my house-mates.'

Camilla's blue eyes shone like sapphires in the pale beauty of her face. She tossed back her black curly hair and treated Jed to one of her most theatrical smiles.

'*Enchantée*, darling!'

'Hi.' Jed's handshake was coolly polite. He turned back to Ana, with a half-smile which contained a decidedly mocking gleam. 'Goodnight, Ana. I'll buy you two glasses of wine tomorrow. We'll take it from there.'

Colour surged into her face.

'Like hell we will,' she spat, through clenched teeth. 'Goodnight, Jed.'

'Don't forget to keep your door locked,' he advised smoothly. Without a wave, he loped athletically downstairs. There was a decisive click of the latch as he let himself out.

'Come on, Ana, darling, *tell*!' Camilla was settling down on Ana's bed for a delicious gossip session. 'Who is he, what's the story?'

Ana found she was weak at the knees. Shakily she sat down on the pile of clothes, and glared bleakly at her friend.

'He's—he's—well, I suppose he's an old . . . friend,' she managed finally. 'A—a friend of my father's, you could say . . .'

'You don't sound very sure,' Camilla remarked, tucking her legs up beneath her and winding a black curl thoughtfully round her index finger. 'Either he is or he isn't!'

Ana gazed at her blankly. The confusion she'd felt with Jed's powerful presence dominating her emotions had been bad enough. But this acute agitation now he'd gone was guaranteed to keep her awake half the night...

Tomorrow was Sunday. She had no performances at the theatre as an excuse to hide away from him. Maybe she could get up at the crack of dawn and catch a bus somewhere, anywhere?

'He's an ex-friend,' she heard herself saying dismissively. 'It didn't work out, and it never will. He's not my type at all...'

To underline the statement, she stood up and stretched, loosening the strained muscles of her neck and shoulders. To hide her eyes from her friend's eagle gaze, she dropped her chin to her chest, rolled her head from one shoulder to the other, then lowered her upper half towards the floor, hanging there in the classic relaxation position. Her hair fell in a thick blonde curtain around her head.

'You mean, if I took a liking to him, you wouldn't mind?' Camilla purred.

'Go ahead,' Ana said in a muffled voice. Slowly straightening up, she attempted a smile which felt more like a grimace. 'Be my guest. Lord, I'm tired, Camilla. Do you mind if I throw you out and get to bed?'

'No. I'm going.' Camilla paused at the door, and flashed a teasing grin before she disappeared. 'But that wasn't one of your most convincing performances. From where I was standing, Jed Steele looked very much your type, darling! 'Night!'

Alone, Ana gazed distantly around the room, then automatically began to shrug off her clothes and get ready for bed. Camilla was too perceptive. And she was right. Jed Steele had been, all too briefly, the one man Ana had ever met who filled every one of her dreams, made her feel excited and special, and floating, and deliciously feminine, and...

And he'd hurt her more than any other man. Led her on, urged her up to a dizzy, ecstatic height of wanting, and then ruthlessly dropped her, walked away. She paused in the act of scrubbing her teeth, catching sight of herself in the bathroom mirror. Wide brown eyes gazed back, startlingly dark against the natural blonde of her hair. She took after her father. He was grey now, but he had the same dark eyes, and his hair had been the same shade of blond...

After a quick shower, and with the battered teddy propped on the chair with the discarded clothes, she climbed into bed in her white, pin-tucked cotton chambray nightshirt, and made a mental note to tidy her room tomorrow. It was her Sunday job. Sunday was the only day she had any free time to do anything in. The sooner she got to sleep, the sooner she could wipe Jed Steele from her mind...

But as she lay there in the darkness Jed Steele filled her mind. His reappearance had robbed her of any peace. She could do nothing to stop the memories from rolling back and crushing her...

CHAPTER TWO

IT WAS early when Ana finally woke up. Unforgivably early for a Sunday morning. Her duvet and pillow had somehow parted company with the bed during her stormy, restless night. They lay haphazardly on the floor beside her. Feeling shivery and unrefreshed, she carefully remade the bed as a determined start to her Sunday domesticity. Then she pushed her feet into padded crimson towelling slippers, hugged her matching dressing-gown round herself, and went blearily downstairs to make a cup of tea.

The house was silent, as she'd expected it to be. If Camilla, Pru or David, her fellow residents, heard her moving around at half-past eight they'd doubtless think they were dreaming, pull their covers over their heads and burrow back to sleep again.

In the small, pine-panelled kitchen, she sat as close to the radiator as she could, sipped the steaming mug of strong tea, and gazed out of the window at the misty autumn sunshine breathing life into the patio-style back garden. Last night she'd dreamed almost non-stop, about Jed. Squeezing her eyes shut, she saw pictures from those dreams, vivid and fragmented, but indelible. However hard she tried, she couldn't shut them out. She didn't want to think about him, about the pain he'd caused her, about the fool she'd made of herself. But the details were crowding back into her mind, sharp and tormenting as invisible needles...

That hot July day, four years ago. She'd just finished her first year at LAMDA. A virus had laid her low in the final few weeks of term, and she'd battled on, determined not to miss a single day of her course. When the holidays had finally arrived, she'd abandoned plans to stay with friends, and instead caught the train home to Dorset, to surprise her father.

After the frenetic pace of drama school, she'd been anticipating blissful peace at Farthingley, the sixteenth-century mansion where she'd spent an idyllic childhood. Instead, she'd arrived to find the house and its ancient wooded grounds seething with her father's company employees, manically preparing for a top-level conference.

Her father's secretary-PA had met her in the hall, her cool reception implying that Ana was intruding where she wasn't wanted.

Security was high on the agenda, she'd stated cautiously, eyeing Ana's wind-swept blonde hair, ripped denim jeans and outsized denim shirt with misgivings. While there was no specific cause for alarm, she'd informed Ana, Hart Pharmaceuticals had to take routine precautions against cranks. That was why there was so much coming and going in the house and grounds. Frankly, she was surprised Ana's father had invited her home.

Ana had retreated to the kitchen, coaxed some freshly baked flapjacks and a carton of orange juice from Ellen, snatched the old picnic rug and a straw sunhat from the cupboard, and retired to the tranquillity of the walled herb garden with her well-thumbed copy of *Romeo and Juliet*.

Rounding the clipped, nine-foot yew hedge, preoccupied by childhood memories induced by the heady scent of lavender and rosemary, she'd literally bumped, headlong, into Jed Steele.

A pair of hard brown hands had stabilised her. She'd looked up into that cold grey-green gaze, locked eyes with him for the very first time, and felt... How had she felt? Different. Altered, in some fundamental way. Like emotionally crash-landing in a jungle, without a clue how to hack her way out again...

'Who are you?' he mused, a gleam in his eyes. 'A spy from a rival drugs company, maybe?'

'I *could* be.' She heard her unsteady voice, her husky laugh, and felt mystified.

He hadn't released her. He was still holding her upper arms in a firm grip. She was registering the most extraordinary sensations from the warm touch of his fingers. Even through the blue denim of her shirt, tiny impulses were snaking their way along her nerve-endings, arousing the sensitive army of hormones just beneath the surface of her skin...

She drew a shaky breath, pulling herself together determinedly. She couldn't be feeling this riot of reaction to a chance encounter with a total stranger. Maybe it was the aftermath of her virus.

'I'm not, though,' she added on a calmer note. 'I'm more in favour of alternative medicine. I prefer natural remedies to manufactured ones, don't you?'

It was a provocative question, she knew. This man could only be here as one of her father's employees. He'd hardly admit to siding with the enemy.

'I'll plead the Fifth Amendment on that,' he murmured. There was no visible reaction on the harsh, dark face. This was a characteristic she was to become familiar with. Jed Steele appeared to have trained himself to control his reaction to provocation.

'You'd better identify yourself,' he added coolly.

'Lord above——' she flicked her eyes comically skywards, twisting her arms free of his restraint '—I come home for a spot of peace and quiet, and get interrogated in my own herb garden!'

'You're William French's daughter?' His eyes raked her up and down without the faintest flicker of personal interest. 'Come to think of it, you look like him.'

'Since my father's fifty-something and decidedly rotund, I'm not sure how to take that. And who are *you*?' She widened her brown eyes enquiringly beneath the brim of the ancient straw hat. He looked sober and efficient and business-like, she noted, in a darkly expensive grey suit, white lawn shirt, muted fawn silk tie. In the warmth of the summer afternoon, and in contrast to her own casual attire, he looked over-dressed. There was a portable telephone, or two-way radio receiver, or something, in his pocket.

'Don't tell me...you're Dad's latest right-hand man? The new "company son", eager to impress?'

The level gaze narrowed. Ana felt a jolt of confusion. Why had she said that? The sarcasm, the world-weary air she'd projected hadn't even begun to reflect what she was feeling inside. Resorting to this self-protective act was fine when she *wanted* to fend someone off. But did she *want* to fend off this man?

'And you're his spoilt, bolshie teenage daughter, eager to stir up trouble?' It was more a cool observation than a malicious insult.

She reddened, and bit her lip. With a slight, embarrassed laugh, she said quickly, 'I'm not *spoilt*! Why does everyone always assume that because I'm the only daughter of a very rich man I must be spoilt?'

'Maybe you're not in a position to judge?'

Was there the faintest glimmer of amusement in the cool gaze?

'Maybe not. But then neither are you! You don't know me well enough to judge me,' she reasoned, with a dimpled grin. Gesturing to the picnic basket hooked on her arm, she added impulsively, 'Why don't you join me for a flapjack? We can exchange life stories.'

There was a fractional pause.

'Some other time, maybe.'

He turned go to, and impulsively she said, 'I'm Anastasia—Ana—French. Don't you have a name?'

'Jed Steele.' After a second's deliberation, he turned back and gravely shook her outstretched hand. The wry smile she'd prompted made her heart squeeze and then leap crazily in her chest. With most people, a smile was just a smile. With Jed, it was such a brilliant contrast to the wary hardness of his features that it took her breath away.

She met him again at dinner. He was sitting beside her father, in a darker, more formal evening suit. They appeared to be in deep, soft-voiced conversation. The brilliant smile she gave him was ignored. The cool snub seemed deliberate. She was staggered by the sharp contraction of pain in her stomach...

Without admitting it to herself, she'd taken abnormal care with her appearance—hair piled up in an elegant chignon, subtle make-up to enhance her tilted brown eyes and high cheek-bones, short brown silk skirt and a cropped cream lace blouse.

'You look gorgeous tonight,' her father had announced proudly when Ana had dropped an affectionate kiss on his thick, greying blond hair and joined them at the table. 'Don't you agree, Jed?'

Her father had turned to Jed, with a proud grin. 'Have you met my daughter? Just back from her first year at drama school. She's going to be a famous actress one day!'

'We met earlier, in the garden,' Jed had murmured non-committally, his light grey-green eyes dissecting her appearance with just the faintest hint of sexual interest. Ana had felt goose-bumps shivering the surface of her skin. Suddenly the cream lace top had felt transparent. Her lack of bra had felt like a major indiscretion. Fighting the warm blush creeping into her face, she'd averted her eyes quickly.

There were several of the company directors at dinner that night. The hum of conversation had gradually risen as wine and excellent food were consumed. The old oak-panelled dining-room, the candlelight and the flowers on the long, highly polished refectory table felt familiar yet strangely alien with Jed Steele's cool gaze moving with what struck her as ruthless detachment over the entire gathering...

She pointedly concentrated on relating all her news to her father. She always enjoyed the warmth of his lively interest in her life. In turn, she heard about the conference, about the top-ranking scientists and drug-company chiefs expected to arrive the next morning.

When the meal was over, Jed Steele left the room before everyone else. But, gaining confidence from his absence, her subtle enquiries about the nature of his role in the company drew very little information from her father. Jed was here for the duration of the conference, just a 'temporary assignment', he explained vaguely. That was all she could glean. Her father could be infuriatingly obtuse when he chose to be.

After coffee, leaving them all discussing the final requirements in the big, book-lined library where the conference was to be staged, she strolled out through the French doors, across the wide, sloping lawn towards the rustic summer-house in the far corner.

Dreamily, she breathed in the summer-night smells, the heavy sweetness of roses and honeysuckle. Smelling the flowers made her think of her mother. She'd died when Ana was nine, but she'd been mad on gardening. Ana could remember walking with her in the garden, on a summer's evening. If she could be granted three wishes by some obliging fairy, she'd use all three to wish her mother alive again, to have her here when she came home...

It was dusk. Rapidly getting dark. There was no one around. Impulsively, maybe as an extension of her sad train of thought, she launched softly and passionately into Juliet's speech to Romeo, begging him to stay longer in their secret garden tryst. She was huskily declaiming into the darkness, '"... it is not yet near day: It was the nightingale, and not the lark... Believe me, love, it was the nightingale..."' when a dark figure separated itself from the shadow of the summerhouse. She choked to a halt, with a gasp of fright.

'It's OK, it's only me.' Considering she hardly knew him, Jed's deep, amused voice was oddly reassuring.

Trembling with reaction, she found herself clutching her arms around herself, half laughing, half furious.

'Do you suppose we're doomed to bump into each other in gardens?' Embarrassment made her speak more sharply than she'd intended. 'What are you doing, creeping round out here in the bushes?'

'Same as you?' he suggested neutrally. 'Except I wasn't spouting Shakespeare to myself.'

'You *recognised* it?' she murmured, with reprehensible sarcasm. 'You don't look the type to know any Shakespeare.'

Why, why, *why* was she driven to be so unbearably bitchy towards him? Because his sardonic gaze was making her feel extremely silly? Inwardly wincing, outwardly braced for retaliation, she stared up at him. Tall and motionless, his face in shadow, he was eyeing her up and down slowly. They were standing very close together. An electricity seemed to have invaded the air between them.

A few minutes ago she'd been conscious of the garden, the sounds and scents of the summer evening. A distant hoot of an owl in the woods. Small rustles in the undergrowth. Now she was aware only of him.

'I'd imagine most people would recognise that particular speech from *Romeo and Juliet*. And what "type" looks as if he knows Shakespeare?' he queried, with bleak humour. There was an ominous glitter in his gaze, visible even in the shadowed darkness. 'Should I be wearing an arty beard and a floppy bow-tie?'

Nervously, she took in his appearance. The suit he'd evidently felt to be *de rigueur* at dinner had been swapped for black chinos and a charcoal-grey polo shirt, open at the neck.

'No,' she assured him, unsteadily, 'you look fine as you are...'

The casual outfit made him look slightly less intimidating. The portable phone was still in evidence, hooked on to a dark leather belt at his waist. Whatever this conference-duration role entailed, he obviously took it very seriously, she deduced. Perhaps he had to be alert and ready twenty-four hours a day, to field urgent calls from delegates arriving from Switzerland or Hong Kong or Timbuktu...?

'Sorry...was I interrupting an important rehearsal?' he queried, deadpan.

'I was just strolling in the garden,' she pointed out rather stiffly, 'enjoying the night air. Smelling the roses and...'

'Is that what that perfume is?' There was that teasing, taunting tone in his voice again. For some reason, she sensed that he wasn't talking about the flowers. He'd made no move to touch her, but his eyes seemed to be touching her. The shortness of the brown silk skirt hadn't bothered her before. Now she felt vulnerable, acutely aware of the bare length of her legs. The night air felt cool on her slender thighs. Her underwear—small lacy cream briefs—seemed too skimpy beneath the thin summer clothes. Without quite understanding why, she was beginning to wish she'd donned an all-encasing bodysuit, armoured herself against whatever this man was doing to her emotions...

'It could be mine,' she admitted. Her voice was unrecognisable—husky, strained with suppressed emotion. 'I got rather carried away when I was spraying it on after my shower earlier...' And hadn't she sprayed on a little more, before she came out here after dinner? Just in case she bumped into him again? The small prod of honesty made her blush in the deepening dusk.

The hard mouth twitched as he stared solemnly down at her. Could he read her mind? Had he somehow detected that her effort with her appearance tonight had been inspired by meeting him? It was a humiliating thought, and yet the notion that he was silently mocking her made her feel angry, indignant and rebellious at the same time...

Some demon inside her prompted her to step closer, go on tiptoe in her flat brown leather sandals, steady herself with one tentative hand on his shoulder, and lift her chin so that the slender curve of her neck was exposed.

'It's *Fleurs du Jardin*—do you like it?' She spoke in a light, matter-of-fact tone, but her eyes held his, with a steady challenge. She was inwardly overcome with horror at her audacity, but for the life of her she couldn't stop herself.

Her heart hammering, heat flickering over her skin, she waited as he thoughtfully considered her. Taking her chin in his thumb and forefinger, he twisted her head to the side. Bending slowly, he lowered his head to within a hair's breadth of making contact, and inhaled the sweet warm scent at the hollow of her clavicle.

'Not quite to my taste. A little too... girlish, maybe...'

But his voice had altered. There was a slight thickening in his tone. She stiffened at the subtle put-down. Too *girlish*? How old was he? she wondered indignantly. Around thirty? Mortified, she took a shaky step away from him. She felt a very 'spoilt' urge to slap his face, and suppressed it hastily.

'I'm not a girl, I'm a woman,' she said idiotically.

The green gaze narrowed. A twitch of laughter at the corner of his mouth should have completed her mortification, should have sent her running for the safety of her bedroom, but she felt transfixed, frozen to the spot. Her brain seemed to have frozen too. The only part of her working overtime was her heart, hammering away like an express train. She'd never felt so vulnerable, so emotionally confused, in her life.

There was a hoarse hint of humour and masculine impatience as he spoke again. 'Shouldn't you be going inside to bed, Miss French? Instead of roaming round the gardens trying to seduce strange men with your perfume?'

'Trying to *seduce*...?' She glared at him in stunned humiliation. 'You think I'm trying to seduce you? Your conceit is unbelievable! And if I want to roam round the gardens, well, I can do what I like—I live here!' she finished hotly, in spite of the anxious thud of her heart.

Quite at variance with her words, her pulses were racing frantically. Heat was glowing all over her body. Inwardly, she was appalled at herself. The accuracy of his taunt was unbearable. Just then, stepping closer, inviting him to smell her perfume...what else had she been doing but playing around on the fringes of seduction? But surely more flirtatious than seductive? Did he think she was cheap? That she made a habit of this, God forbid? What was the matter with her? She'd had casual boyfriends since she was about fifteen. She mixed with male students every single day at college. But never before had she felt this frightening pull of attraction. Towards a virtual stranger...

'And you claim you're not spoilt?' The softly laconic goad cut like a whip. 'How old are you, Ana?'

'Nineteen! I've just finished a year at drama school! And I'm not spoilt,' she told him, with husky emphasis. 'Spoilt people are damaged individuals, products of parents with no time for them. My parents always had time for me. My father still has. I can't help it if he's rich! That doesn't mean he's spoiled me!'

Jed Steele's gaze was wry.

'Maybe not,' he drawled, his eyes teasing, 'but would he be proud of you if he could see you now?'

'What do you mean?'

'Throwing yourself at a man you hardly know, in the garden at midnight.'

'I'm doing no such thing——' She opened her mouth to protest, on fire with humiliation, then found herself hauled hard against the full length of his body, and crushed there mercilessly.

'Maybe you need teaching a lesson, little Lolita,' he murmured laconically against the loose, silky chignon of her hair. His breath was warm against her ear. 'The lesson is don't play games.'

'Oh!' The choked gasp was forced out of her as she registered the hardness of his body, lifted her arms to push him away without success. 'Please, let go of me...'

'Let go of you? When you've been busy giving me the come-on since we met this afternoon? Play fair, sweetheart. I'm only human... God, what the hell are you wearing under here?' The taunting, amused growl of sensual discovery made her feel quite faint. Her raised arms had lifted the cropped hem of the lace top, baring a wedge of soft, warm midriff.

'No, please...!' At the touch of his fingers on her naked skin, her strangled shudder was utterly ambiguous. Eyes squeezed tight shut, she was drifting in a torment of self-doubt, outrage, and newly awakened need. She wanted this to stop, right now. And she wanted it to go on and on forever...

She was rigid with shame, but awash with sensation as his hard hands moved irresistibly upwards to caress the narrow expanse of her ribcage, not quite reaching the small, high jut of her breasts, then sweeping down again to mould her close against him.

Her choked moan was neither rejection nor invitation, nor was her convulsive writhe against the heat of his body. But with an abrupt oath he dropped his mouth to plunge his tongue arrogantly between her parted lips. He kissed her with a hungry power that made her head spin, and she found herself kissing him back, shudders of response rippling through her. More incriminating still, as she lifted her arms to cling to his shoulders, the short skirt rode higher. Jed's abrupt sweep of her body terminated in long bare thigh, and the temptation to slide higher to the curves beneath the silk was clearly one he didn't intend to resist...

When his stroking hands became bolder, arrogantly exploring the length of her spine to cup the petite swell of her buttocks in their skimpy triangle of cream lace, crushing her punishingly against the hardening bulge of his own body, fear and self-preservation came to her rescue. Blindly, she wrenched her mouth free, aimed a fiercely furious kick at his shins, and began to thump and pummel his chest with her fists.

'Stop it, *stop* it...!' she was half sobbing in the darkness.

'You're not playing this game any more?' The tersely teasing words were bitten between clenched teeth.

She found herself released unceremoniously.

'OK,' he told her bluntly. His eyes were moving over her dishevelled, distressed state without compunction. 'Tonight's your lucky night, lady. You're dealing with someone who abides by the rules. Usually. Treat that as a lesson in consequences.'

'Consequences...?' She could hardly speak.

'Of your own actions. Save your flirting games for the boys in your drama class, Ana.'

He'd said he'd teach her a lesson—and he had, she reflected bitterly, the tears drying on her white face as he turned and walked away.

And even if he'd left it there, stayed right away from her from then on, it would still have been a lesson she'd never have forgotten...

How had he become so...embittered? Ana wondered now, huddled in the early morning chill of the kitchen, gazing through the spiral of steam from her mug of tea. The promise of another glorious September day was gilding the scene through the window, but she didn't see it. All she could see was that ruthless glitter in Jed's eyes as he'd demonstrated his superior strength, annihilated her self-esteem...

There was nothing soft about Jed Steele. Nothing warm. And by the time he'd finished amusing himself with her that fateful weekend every one of her fragile, youthful emotions seemed to have iced over to match...

The knock at the front door brought her back to the present with a jolt. Nine o'clock. Not an accepted time for callers on a Sunday morning...

Her shock at seeing Jed, calmly standing on the doorstep, was swiftly followed by horror at the state she was in. Pale and sleepy, hair wildly awry, the crimson dressing-gown bundled round her anyhow, she glared at him furiously. He looked impossibly attractive, in close-fitting Levis, white shirt and thick-ribbed navy jersey. A soft fawn suede jacket was slung over his shoulders. In daylight, the crisp, wind-ruffled brown hair had subtle gold-bronze lights in it. The cool green gaze and strong, tanned features were even more painfully familiar.

'Not *you* again!' she managed, raking an unsteady hand through her hair.

'Can I come in?'

He didn't wait for an answer. Overpoweringly blocking the hall, he eyed her up and down wryly.

'I had some interesting dreams last night. How about you?'

'Mine were nightmares,' she supplied shortly. 'What do you want, Jed?'

'I came to find out what actresses do on Sundays.'

'This one usually sleeps in late, then catches up on the jobs she hasn't had time to do in the week.'

'I hope I didn't get you out of bed?' He didn't sound particularly repentant.

'No. I was awake.'

'Bacon, eggs and coffee would go down well.'

'Jed, I really...'

He'd strolled into the kitchen, and was investigating the decidedly sketchy contents of the fridge and larder.

'Go and get dressed, Ana,' he ordered with a grin, shutting the fridge door with a slight shake of his head. 'I'll take you out for breakfast.'

'I don't *want* to go out for breakfast.'

'Well, I do. And I didn't forgo the full English version at my hotel to make do with half a bowl of cornflakes and a slice of mouldy toast. So move it.'

Her jaw dropped, but suddenly words failed her. Curiosity, strong, potent and dangerous, had begun to consume her. Whatever had brought Jed determinedly back into her life, he appeared to have some purpose. And she might have grown a protective shell these last four years, but the sight of Jed lounging nonchalantly in her small kitchen, professing a desire to eat breakfast with her, was more than her embattled defences could stand.

'OK,' she agreed flatly, swinging out of the door to hide her eyes from that probing, all-seeing gaze. 'If having breakfast with you is what it takes to get rid of you, fine. Breakfast it is. *Just* breakfast...'

'Just breakfast,' Jed agreed easily. But something in the wry tone of his voice made the soft hairs all over her body prickle into red alert...

CHAPTER THREE

THE short drive to Jed's hotel was accomplished in chilly silence. He was staying in one of the most luxurious hotels in the town, a half-timbered Elizabethan affair set in its own grounds. The dining-room was elegant, overlooking the river. Pale green damask cloths adorned the tables, with china bowls of russet chrysanthemums.

While Jed calmly consumed bacon, sausage, egg, fried bread and grilled tomatoes, Ana tried valiantly to do the same. But she was too tense to eat. To avoid eye contact, she kept her eyes on the view through the small leaded-light windows. The tranquil River Avon flowed very close by. She could see sunlit willows across the river, stroking the water with their lacy branches. A swan glided by, its beady eyes scanning the banks for tourists bearing bread.

'Eat your breakfast,' he ordered, shooting her a bleak grin.

'I did tell you I wasn't hungry.'

'So you did.' Leaning back in his chair, he scanned her impassively. Wriggling slightly under that cool scrutiny, she gazed about the room. There were guests at several of the tables near by. An American couple, and Germans, French and

Japanese, Ana deduced, from the rich blend of languages and accents. Part of the ever-present pageant of tourists, flocking to experience Shakespeare's county, to absorb the atmosphere left by the centuries. Stratford's lure for visitors from so many different countries and cultures never failed to give her a warm little glow of pleasure.

Until now. Right now, she could think of nothing except devising some casual, uninterested-sounding excuse to escape from Jed's company...

'You look tired, Ana,' he murmured, pushing his knife and fork together and lifting a hand to summon the waiter. 'I imagine acting is an exhausting profession?' There was no expression in his voice.

'It can be very tiring,' she agreed equally tonelessly. The waiter poured more tea into her cup, topped up Jed's black coffee, then disappeared obediently in search of more toast. 'You don't get much time off. But I love it...'

'When did you last take a holiday?'

She shrugged slightly, irritation creeping in. 'Heavens, I can't remember. I've got a free ten-day slot coming up soon, I think. Another play's preview week. But it's possible to do the entire season without a holiday. It's just the luck of the draw.'

'Is that why you're looking like the walking dead?'

'*Spare* me the flowery compliments!' she snapped. 'If you must know I'm feeling... stunned! I can't believe I'm seeing you again!' Horrified, she heard herself blurting it out. 'I thought I never would. See you again, I mean. Part of it is like a nightmare. Part of it feels more like a dream. A dream I've had on and off since that weekend at Farthingley...'

She caught her lip in her teeth, mortified. So much for her urgent desire to play it cool, to escape.

'I've thought about Farthingley, too.' His deep voice was guarded.

Her face felt hot. Beneath her loose, scoop-necked emerald sweatshirt, her breasts tingled, the tips traitorously tightened like press-studs.

How could he still make her feel like this? Fighting the waves of heat, she struggled angrily to examine her subconscious feelings. Trying to make sense of her reaction to him felt like agitating muddy water with a stick. Hadn't she hated him, despised him, resented him, blamed him for her sexual hang-ups, for the last four years? Burned with mortification, whenever she remembered that rejection on the lawn, and then the second, even more devastating rejection, the later episode she could hardly bear to relive? Was she so weak that she could sit here now, bleating on about dreams, as if he could still mean something to her?

'I don't believe you.'

'No. I guess you wouldn't.'

She fixed him with an intense brown gaze.

'Unless it was to think back and gloat?' she suggested tightly. 'Presumably you got quite a kick out of that weekend?'

Jed's face had darkened.

'I was doing a job that weekend.'

'Oh, yes, the mysterious "job". The one which entailed prowling round with portable phones and two-way radios and pouncing on innocent girls practising their Shakespeare in the garden?'

'I didn't pounce on you, Ana. Wasn't it the other way around?' The smooth taunt was so cruelly familiar, she felt the colour drain from her face.

She stood up abruptly, then felt Jed's fingers catch her forearm, restraining her with easy strength.

'Hey, loosen up,' he advised softly. 'We're raking over the ashes of something that never even happened.'

'*What*?' She couldn't help it. Suddenly she was quivering with breathless outrage. 'You—you practically scar me for life, then say it never happened?'

His eyes narrowed. Slowly he stood up too and moved around the table so that he could hold on to her more forcibly.

'What the hell are you talking about, Ana?'

'I'm talking about being treated like a—a *whore*,' she shot back unsteadily, uncaring of the surprised glances twisting their way, 'then...humiliated...rejected in the...the most callous way possible, by someone I'd *imagined* might be my *hero!*'

'Your hero?' he echoed. The amusement had faded to a bleak, lingering mockery, needling her into fresh fury. 'How the hell did you imagine I might be your hero, Ana? You didn't know the first thing about me!'

'No. And I learned my lesson, didn't I? Oh, I can't believe I'm even *talking* to you!' With all her strength, she twisted free of his hand, and stalked out of the dining-room, oblivious to the minor stir she'd created in her wake.

Jed caught up with her outside. He grabbed her arm, spun her round with rough insistence. Unwillingly, she stared up at his dark, tense features, the hard brilliance of his eyes.

'Ana, you're not making any sense.'

'No, maybe not,' she managed, more evenly. She had her wayward emotions under control for the moment.

'Maybe a passion for drama implies a capacity for melodrama?'

'Can we just forget it?'

'Not easy. We need to talk,' he grinned, his voice husky. He was frogmarching her down towards the river, ignoring her angry writhings to free herself.

'Let go of me, Jed.'

'Ana, calm down——'

'I won't calm down. Let me go or I'll scream.'

With a curt, distinctly vulgar epithet, he jerked her into his arms, restraining her furious struggles. They'd reached the gardens down by the river, and they were standing in the path of a large group of Japanese tourists, who were busily photographing everything in sight. The whirr of cameras and excited, animated discussion was suddenly all around them. Apparently oblivious, Jed twisted her chin up in his fingers, and silenced her irate protests by kissing her, hard and long, on her trembling mouth.

The outside world receded. The only focus of energy was the heat and demand of Jed's touch.

'I'd forgotten how good you taste,' he breathed hoarsely, lifting his head a fraction to inspect her stunned face.

'Jed, please don't——' It was a whisper, choked back into her mouth as he dropped a slow, lazy, sensual kiss on her lips then outlined the soft oval of her parted lips with his tongue, before thrusting deeply inside again. His skill, his sensual arrogance was provoking a meltdown of desire she could scarcely control...

'Ana...sweet little Ana—God, I'm so sorry...' The husky words were breathed, almost inaudible against her lips. But the sensations he was arousing were too forceful to ignore. The light cotton jersey fabric of her emerald-green top and stretchy black leggings was woefully inadequate as protection. From her breasts, crushed against the iron-hard muscle of his chest, to her stomach, moulded with outrageous intimacy to his groin, to her thighs, tightly pressed to the rough denim of his legs, she was in flames. On fire, but shivering, all over. Melting, burning up. Only the belated recollection that they were embracing in a very public place brought her back to her senses ...

'Jed, *please* ... !' The anguish in her whisper seemed to get through to him. Slowly, he lessened the pressure on her spine, freed her from the heat of his body.

'We'll take a rowing-boat out on the river.' The flat statement should have triggered an indignant argument. It said a great deal for the weakening after-effects of Jed's assault on her that she allowed herself to be led, without a word of protest, down to the boat-yard ...

Huddled in the corner of the boat, hugging her knees in mute self-defence, she watched him rowing. He did this effortlessly, as she might have imagined he would. The navy jersey had been slung off, and the shirt beneath, baggy-cut and long-sleeved, looked like silk. An expensive, impeccably cut, foreign-looking silk. The ripple of the dark, powerful body beneath the fine white fabric had a profound effect on her senses.

'What do you want, Jed?' She managed to form the question, although the explicit way he'd just kissed her had left her in little doubt.

'Right now?' he teased softly. 'Best not to ask.'

'Sex, at a crude guess?' she forced out, with a small laugh. 'And you're arrogant enough to think you can just call in on your way through Stratford, and pick up what you discarded a few years ago?'

'I wanted to take you to bed four years ago.' He shot a bitterly humorous glance her way. 'And I still do. But it wasn't that simple then, and it's not that simple now.'

Ana closed her eyes. There was a charged, panicky feeling tightening her muscles, sending small, soft shivers up and down her spine. She let one trembling hand drift over the side of the small wooden rowing-boat. The cold, silken, greenish water of the Avon trailed over her fingers.

'I want to know. Is that why you're here, Jed?' she demanded shakily. 'To attend to unfinished business?'

There was a silence. She opened her eyes. The boat had slowed, and bumped gently to a halt. Jed had pulled over towards a deserted stretch of bank where the willows shivered their slender branches in the wind. Through their leaves the hazy autumn sunshine and the river fragmented into a mosaic of greyish blue and gold.

'Like I said. I wish it were that simple...'

'So that's a no? You're not really arrogant enough to think you could just march back into my life and haul me into bed with you?'

'No.' Jed's expression was guardedly amused.

'Just as well. If you'd said yes, I'd have tipped you in the river!'

'Don't waste your strength trying.'

'You think I couldn't?'

He grinned at her, lazy speculation in his eyes. 'I know you couldn't.'

She fenced silent glares with him for a few seconds, then clenched her fists in her lap, drawing a deep breath to control her temper.

There was a long, thoughtful silence. Something shuttered, coolly evasive in Jed's eyes made her heart contract. Another mystery? she wondered bitterly. More secrets? Unanswered questions? What *was* it about this man? Was he so congenitally lacking in self-confidence that he had to fabricate a dark cloak of illusion around himself? But it would be hard to visualise Jed lacking self-confidence. It oozed from him as powerfully as his sexuality, and his cynicism.

'Maybe we've both had different versions of what happened four years ago,' he drawled wryly. He'd tied the boat loosely to a low-hanging willow branch. They were marooned in a small, watery oasis of peace. The contrast of outer tranquillity and inner turmoil was intensely ironic, Ana reflected, her head spinning.

'You think so?' she managed at last.

'It seems that way to me.' Jed's lidded gaze was swamping her senses. 'You say you saw me as a kind of hero. What are we talking here? Knights on white chargers? Princes in fairy-tales?'

'I wouldn't waste my breath trying to explain,' she snapped in a small, cold voice. 'I was much younger. Still—still a child in many ways, and...'

'You assured me you were a woman,' he teased softly.

Colour flared in her cheeks. Pressing the soft fullness of her lips into an angry, defensive line, she sent him a look of pure hatred.

'I don't even remember much about it all,' she lied raggedly.

'You seem to have heroes and knights in armour slightly muddled up in your head,' he added softly. 'I wanted you that night in your bedroom, Ana. Do you think it was easy, backing off like that? Finding you were a virgin?'

'If you call it heroic, leading me on and then rejecting me on some...some feeble excuse about not messing around with virgins,' she flared, her sarcasm hiding her pain, 'then you're the one who's confused!'

'You knew nothing about me, Ana.' It was a grim reproof.

With a surge of embarrassment, she drew her knees up closer, and hugged them tighter, turning her cheek and resting her head so that her face was hidden.

'That's not true. I—I knew my father had great respect for you, whatever it was you were doing for him. And we talked, that evening, after the conference, didn't we?'

'Oh, yes,' he mocked gently. 'You mean, when you cooked me tagliatelle and we discussed shared tastes in pasta, country pubs and Pavarotti?'

The memory of that weekend still hurt, like a physical wound. After Friday night's episode by the summer-house, he'd managed a guarded kind of apology on the Sunday night. Idiotically, in spite of everything, there'd been a fragile blossoming of her emotions again. A brief illusion of rapport, lifting her hopes. Wishful thinking, of course. A figment of her fevered imagination. And then the crash back down to earth. There'd been a power cut, some chaos, and Jed had ended up in her bedroom and she'd ended up making the ultimate fool of herself...

'I know it's laughable now. At the time, it just felt... it just felt... right,' she whispered, with a bleak laugh. 'Don't worry, Jed, I've grown out of it. Out of the—the youthful infatuation part, that is...'

'So what's left?' The wry probe made her tense inwardly.

'Virtually nothing!'

'So I imagined the shivers of response, when I kissed you?' The deep voice was so soft, she could only just make out the words. Catching her breath, she squeezed her eyes shut in despair. This couldn't be happening to her. This cool, male dissection of her innermost feelings...

'Jed,' she managed at last, lifting her chin and meeting his lidded eyes with a steady gaze, 'this is *not* going to work. Do you understand?'

'What isn't?'

'Don't be deliberately *obtuse*!' she said coldly. '*This—us—*you and me, getting together again! Whatever you've come for, I'd prefer it if you went away again. As quickly as possible. OK?'

There was a long silence. Jed lifted his arms in a lazy stretch, and cupped his hands behind his neck.

'You're getting agitated again,' he said lightly. 'It must be the actress in you. You over-react too much.'

'Look——'

'Have you seen your father recently?' he continued, ignoring her taut interruption. 'Last time I spoke to him, he was worried you were working too hard. I'd say he's right. You're stressed out, Ana. You need a break.'

'I do not need a break.' She struggled with her temper. 'I just need to be left in peace to get on with my career!'

'How about showing me round Stratford?' he suggested casually, untying the boat, and beginning to row them back down the river. 'I'm here for a few days. Warwickshire is all new to me. I can't leave without seeing Shakespeare's birthplace, can I?'

'There are plenty of signposts to it,' she retorted, hugging her arms round herself miserably. 'I've got jobs to do back at the house...'

'What jobs?'

'I've got to tidy my room...' It was a feeble-sounding excuse, and she knew it.

'You can do that later. I'll help you.' The sheer audacity of this suggestion took her breath away. Abruptly, she clamped her mouth shut. It was hopeless, fencing with him. She got too agitated. He was right. Best to stay cool, she reminded herself for the hundredth time.

'I'll take over the rowing,' she said flatly, moving to indicate that she meant it. She felt a sudden, urgent need for physical exertion.

'Will you show me round Stratford, Ana?' He relinquished his position without argument, watching her with lazy amusement as she began to pull hard on the oars, the tip of her tongue between her teeth.

'OK,' she agreed tautly. She hauled hard against the resistance of the water, her eyes on the distant bridge. 'I'll show you round Stratford. Today. If you promise me you'll go and sightsee somewhere else tomorrow.'

'I don't make deals,' he drawled. The taunting light in his eyes deepened her mounting sense of foreboding.

By early evening, Ana felt on the point of near-collapse. They'd seen every half-timbered

Elizabethan building in a twenty-mile radius, or so it seemed. They'd seen where Shakespeare was born, where his parents lived, where he'd lived when he married, and dozens of other places of interest dredged up from some convenient guidebook Jed had produced. The autumn sun had shone benignly, and the brooding beauty of the old buildings had doubtless been remarkable. But she'd never appreciated quite how exhausting the tourist trail could be, especially combined with the emotional tension of being continually in Jed's company.

'I've kept my side of the bargain!' she informed Jed wearily, kicking off her flat black leather ankle boots and swinging her feet up beside her on the leather chesterfield in the hotel lounge, 'so I take it you're leaving in the morning?'

'Bargain?' he teased. 'What bargain was this?'

'The bargain that if I humoured you you'd go away?' she reminded him sweetly.

'I said no deal.' He grinned. Unrepentantly, he raked a thoughtful hand through his thick brown hair. 'I've no intention of going anywhere until I've watched all three plays you're in next week.'

She glared at him, eyes wider.

'You're planning on staying all week?'

'I'm touched by your enthusiasm.'

She groaned, and squeezed her eyes shut.

'Are you OK?'

'Fine. Just after-effects of a full day's foot-slogging round the tourist sights. I thought I was fit but I ache all over!'

'It was the rowing that made you ache. You need a hot bath before you stiffen up.'

'Forget it. Camilla and Pru, not to mention David, will have used up every last drop of hot water by now.'

'Instant solution. Use the bath upstairs in my room.'

'What?' She was instantly wary. 'No way!'

Jed stood up, and reached to take hold of her hands, pulling her up too.

'I'm suggesting you use my bath, not fling yourself naked into my bed, Ana. What are you frightened of?' His hard mouth was mocking. 'Me? Or yourself?'

Both, she wanted to say. But admitting to either would be incriminating. Her heart thudding, she struggled with the decision. If she refused the offer, she risked giving him the wrong impression, didn't she? Risked letting him know how deeply he still affected her. This afternoon they'd walked and talked together as friends, casual acquaintances. They'd even laughed at jokes, relaxed enough to share the funny side of situations they'd encountered. The brief flare of sexual attraction had seemed to take a back seat. The notion of a gloriously hot, deep hotel bath clinched the silent argument.

'Neither,' she assured him with commendable composure. 'As long as your bathroom has a lock on the door.'

'It has,' he assured her smoothly. But the dark gleam in his eyes was far from reassuring.

The bathroom *en suite* with Jed's hotel room was unashamedly luxurious. An enormous white claw-foot bath took pride of place in the centre of the room. Gold taps, huge jungly plants, piles of soft amber towels, and a deep, velvety brown carpet. Safely locked in, and immersed up to her neck in magnolia-scented bubbles, her hair in a loose topknot, Ana took a few moments to examine exactly what was happening to her. Since Jed's reappearance in her life last night, feelings she'd considered to be absolute seemed to be undergoing a subtle sea-change.

It was one thing telling herself she wanted him to go away again. Hurling insults at him. Professing total lack of interest. But she wasn't normally easily led. If she chose not to do something, she didn't do it.

So who was she trying to fool? If she hadn't wanted to come out for the day with Jed, she'd have refused. If she'd had an ounce of sense left, she'd have run a mile just now, when he offered her the use of his hotel bathroom.

The water began to cool around her, and she swished her small, straight toes up through the bubbles, and wriggled them, unseeingly. The muscular aches had gone, but in their place was an ache in her heart. She *was* afraid. Of herself. And of Jed. She wasn't just afraid. She was terrified.

Whatever motive had brought him in search of her, she had excellent reasons for mistrusting it. Four years ago, he'd shown himself to be a hardened cynic, capable of brutal disregard for her feelings and emotions...

That night of the power cut, when he'd come to her room, and things had got out of hand...

She shivered, in spite of the warm water. Didn't he have any idea how much he'd hurt her? Presumably not. Was he so insensitive that he genuinely thought he'd done her a favour in walking out the way he had...?

Climbing out of the bath into the steamed-up atmosphere, she wrapped herself in a huge fluffy bath-sheet, rubbed herself vigorously dry, and pulled on her clothes again. The thought of emerging in the green towelling bathrobe provided struck her as tempting fate to an unwise degree.

'Sorry to hog the bathroom for so long,' she said brightly, emerging to find Jed lounging on the wide blue and peach four-poster bed, reading the Sunday papers. The light outside was beginning to fade slightly. Someone had come in and left a tray of tea and cakes on the table in the window, and lit a log fire in the elegant Minster fireplace. A soft, peach-shaded table lamp had been switched on either side of the bed.

The scene was so alluringly warm and seductive, she stiffened defensively.

'No problem. I took a shower in a spare bathroom along the landing. Did you fall asleep?'

'No. I was just doing some thinking...'

She looked at him properly, and felt her heart contract with a small, warning jerk. His hair was still wet, slicked back. He'd dressed again, in the worn, tight-fitting denims, but he'd swapped the white silk shirt for a black polo-neck. His feet were bare. For a few mesmerised seconds, she found herself thinking that she'd never seen such good-looking feet. Smooth-soled, high-instepped, the toes well-shaped and strong, his skin darkly tanned. Was he always brown? Was it his natural colouring or did he sunbathe regularly in some exotic country? Or use sunbeds? How little she knew about him, she acknowledged, with an unpleasant jolt back to reality...

'Let's have tea, shall we?' he suggested easily, swinging long legs off the bed and coming around to steer her to the tea-table.

'Jed, I should be going. Thanks all the same...'

She made an airy gesture with her arm, and turned towards the door, but he was there before her, blocking her way.

'Stay and have tea, Ana,' he said quietly.

A tension had invaded the air. She opened her mouth, but idiotically no words came out. Almost simultaneously, Jed stepped up to her and hooked her towards him, tightening one hand in the small of her back to crush her to his body, twisting the other into her hair, which collapsed out of its chaotic topknot and cascaded down past her shoulders.

'Tea?' she whispered bleakly, shivering convulsively.

'Yeah, tea,' he assured her, thrusting a muscular, denim-clad knee between her shaking legs, and silencing her muffled protest with his mouth. The onslaught was expert and devastating. Her brief, furious struggle switched, bewilderingly, into a frantic reaction to his touch.

She found herself lifted and deposited on the bed without ceremony, then trapped there while Jed explored the contours of her body with an air of possessive triumph which was frightening and arousing at the same time.

'You promised...' she managed, gasping for breath. Her senses were spinning with dizzy desire, her thighs dissolving. Savage, frighteningly primitive responses surged through her body. She should be fighting—she *had* been fighting, hadn't she? So why now was this urgent need blanking out her defences?

'I promised nothing—I never do,' Jed growled against her ear, biting the small, fleshy lobe with audacious humour. He was peeling up the emerald sweatshirt, circling the high, firm curve of her breasts with the palms of his hands. 'But four years ago I promised myself I'd somehow be rewarded for my self-control, Ana. The reward is now, sweetheart ...'

'Oh, *Jed* ...!' She choked his name, half sobbing, half moaning. 'Don't—please don't do this...'

'Hush, Ana—this is real, not the romantic fantasy performance you wanted before...' The throb of humour and desire was a seductive mixture. His voice had deepened, thickened with need. In spite of all her good intentions, her stomach hollowed with longing.

The black leggings were stretchy, and Jed impatiently pushed them down and hauled them right off, exposing the inadequate protection of cream lace bikini pants, and the vulnerable slimness of long, bare thighs. With one powerful shrugging movement he'd dispensed with his black polo-neck, revealing a disturbing expanse of hard, muscular, golden-tanned torso. She writhed as he slid questing fingers along the inside of her thigh, traced around the delicate hollow of her groin. With unconscious sensuality, she ran her fingers into his hair, arched blindly towards him as he sucked and licked at the sharp ache of her nipples. When he stroked his fingers erotically beneath the silky lace of her panties, she tensed from head to toe, heard herself moan with despairing pleasure...

Part of her wanted him now, more than she'd ever wanted anything before in her life. That part was shivering and melting, burning up with impatient surrender. She felt faint with hunger for the feel of his hands on every secret inch of her body... But another part, the part bruised and damaged by the past, was screaming in silent warning. While the physical pleasure grew higher and higher, the denial grew stronger.

'Do you still want me?' He was shuddering with barely controlled passion as he pinned her to the bed. 'Tell me, Ana...say the words, sweetheart...'

'No...*no*!' Her voice was shaky. The sensation that he was losing control, that he wanted her as fiercely as she wanted him, was a powerful aphrodisiac. Her senses swam, convulsed with desire.

But the touch of his finger, peeling away her last covering, and exploring the hot, damp secrets between the soft, dark blonde curls at the juncture of her legs, brought back all the pain of that first, brutal rejection. She writhed blindly, splayed her hands against the heat of his chest, her emotions raggedly lurching from one extreme to the other. She must be honest. The truth was vital, she dimly acknowledged. But the truth was confused, elusive. A refracted flicker of light at the end of a long, dark, obscure tunnel of doubt.

And then she knew. She understood what was tightening her muscles, contracting her limbs, fighting to preserve her privacy. She couldn't let him *know*! How could she suffer the humiliation of Jed Steele's discovering that no one, since that emotional aberration four years ago, had got close enough to reveal the ultimate mystery...?

Heat swept through her, like a wall of fire. It was unthinkable. Amid all the swamping sensations, this surfaced like a fireball into her conscious mind...

'Stop it, *stop*, Jed!' she sobbed, furious with him, with herself, and with the situation. She contracted herself into a tense ball of denial, pushing at him with hysterical urgency. 'I don't want you—I never shall! So leave me alone! Go away, get out of my life, and leave me *alone*...!'

The urgency, the sincerity of her outburst was absorbed. With an abrupt, muted groan of rueful frustration, he levered himself away, and collapsed, face down, on the bed beside her. Tears welled and trickled down her cheeks, soaked the hair at her temples. She felt too enervated to move her hands to wipe them away.

The phone by the bed shrilled loudly into the silence. Jed, after a few moments' stillness, sat up and grabbed the receiver.

'Jared Steele. Yes...' Something, some change in the atmosphere, made her slowly turn her head on the pillow as he spoke in a low, expressionless voice. He flicked a shuttered glance at her. 'Yes. She's safe. She's fine. That's OK. Yes, as a matter of fact, I do. She's here, with me....'

With an oblique look, Jed passed her the phone. The expression on his face was so reminiscent of that vigilant, immovable face from the past that she felt her stomach sink. Uncertainly she scrubbed her hand over her swollen eyes, and sat up. Something was wrong. Something was strange, definitely odd. She frowned at Jed in bewilderment. Her heart had begun to thump very hard against her ribs.

'For me?' she queried huskily, taking the receiver in nerveless fingers. 'But who on earth would know I was here...?'

'Your father.' Jed's cool eyes made her clutch her arm across her breasts in an agony of humiliation. 'He's got something he needs to tell you, Ana...'

CHAPTER FOUR

'DAD?' Suddenly, despite being naked on Jed's four-poster bed, and reeling from a storm of suppressed, and very adult emotions, she felt like a small child again. 'Daddy? What is it? What's going on?'

'Sweetheart, I didn't want to panic you.' Her father's voice sounded gruff and very unhappy at the other end of the line. 'I've been getting kidnap threats——'

'Someone's trying to kidnap you?' She gasped in horror, but her father gave a humourless laugh.

'Not me, darling. You.'

The breath left her lungs in a rush. Stunned, motionless, she held the receiver to her ear. She tried to concentrate on listening to her father's explanations, but her brain wouldn't function...

Jed had gone to the bathroom, and returned with the dark green towelling robe, wrapping it around her shoulders as her father's rasping, insistent voice continued at the other end of the line.

'I don't belive this,' she interrupted hoarsely as she abruptly registered what she was being told. Jerking her head up, she stared at Jed in wide-eyed disbelief. 'Jed—Jed Steele ...? You're telling me Jed Steele is a professional *body-guard*?'

As she said it, all trace of expression faded from the dark face watching her. The eyes on her were darker, unfathomable. An implacable stranger seemed to replace the man she'd just feverishly responded to on the bed...

He'd crossed the room to stand by the fire, leaning against the chimneypiece. That cool, contained aura was back with a vengeance. He was still naked from the waist up. The faded, snugly fitting Levis moulded the lean hips and cupped around the male bulge of his sex, which curved with disturbing fullness beneath the button-fly fastening. Flames from the logs were flickering cheerfully now, throwing long shadows around the low-ceilinged, black-beamed room. The firelight gleamed on him, playing over broad shoulders, gilding the hard planes of muscle on his chest, arms and abdomen. Dry-mouthed, she found her eyes trapped by the sheer magnetism of his physique, as well as the force of his personality...

Had she somehow fallen asleep, and stepped into a waking dream? she speculated idiotically. Of all the roles she'd played, all the characters she'd portrayed, none had seemed anything like as outlandish or unbelievable as this situation her father was urgently outlining to her.

'Steele's the best,' William French was saying, his voice anxious and abrupt. 'I don't pay out good money for half measures. I've no time for mediocrity, and you know it. And make no mistake. This kidnap threat could be very real. The last thing I intended was to worry you. That's why I asked Steele to keep an eye on you. Without alarming you in any way.' Her father cleared his throat, with a trace of dry humour. 'And he seems to have devised a neat way of doing so, if I read the situation correctly, my dear?'

'I doubt if you do,' she said in a low voice.

Anger was growing, as well as apprehension and alarm and dozens of other emotions she hadn't yet analysed.

Kidnap? Someone was threatening to *kidnap* her? It didn't seem to make any sense. Who would want to kidnap her? And why, if they *did* want to kidnap her, would they inform her father in advance? Wasn't it normally done the other way round?

The brutal truth about Jed's mystery reappearance last night abruptly sank in. She almost felt her heart shrivel in her chest. Jed Steele hadn't waited by the stage door to renew acquaintance. He wasn't remotely interested in their brief, abortive episode four years ago. Hadn't he revealed as much, in the things he'd said today? It had meant so little to him, he'd seemed genuinely amazed that she remembered it at all.

The mysteries clicked into place now, with awful clarity. Jed Steele must have been guarding her father, that weekend four years ago. From whatever threats might have been issued by the 'cranks' his secretary had mentioned . . . ?

And now . . . now he was being paid by her father, to come to Stratford, to make sure she wasn't kidnapped?

A sick, agonising pain was knifing its way through her. How right she'd been to resist the devastating temptation just now! What a cheap, foolish, idiotic thing she would have done, if she'd let her hormones rule her head . . .

The bitterness sweeping through her was so intense, she hardly heard any more of her father's words. And Jed's cool surveillance from across the room was deeply unnerving. She hugged the robe around herself, and wished she could die . . .

'Ana, are you still there, darling?'

'Yes. Yes, I'm here . . . and Dad, I don't *want* Jed Steele to be my—*bodyguard*!' She spat the last word with soft distaste, thrusting a distraught hand through her tousled blonde hair. 'I'd—I'd rather be kidnapped!'

There was a short, charged silence.

'Listen, my girl, if your mother could hear you talk like that, she'd turn in her grave!' William French growled down the line. 'God forbid that you've turned into the spoiled brat your mother and I did our damnedest to avoid . . .'

'Dad . . .' She bit her lip, shame catching her by the throat.

'Let me finish. Jed Steele is the *best*. That's why he was protecting me that weekend at Farthingley, when you met him. I'd had death threats. I didn't tell you, because I didn't want to worry you. Jed kept his role quiet to play down bad publicity for the company. But this man is an international agent. He's guarded kings, Ana. Prime ministers, princes, presidents, you name it . . .'

'Quite the *hero*, then,' she murmured acidly, catching Jed's eye and sending him a look of pure loathing. 'An absolute knight in shining armour. For the right *price*, of course.'

'That's it. He's expensive, but worth every last dollar, darling. Just do as he says. You'll have to quit the theatre, of course——'

'*No*!' Her response was so vehement, she heard her father's intake of breath. 'No, are you crazy?'

'Ana——'

'Dad, have you any idea what being a member of the Royal Shakespeare Company means to my career? How incredibly lucky I was to be chosen? Ask me to do anything, anything else, and I'll do it. But I'm not quitting my contract with the RSC. I might as well write off my career for good, if I did that——'

Jed had come over as she spoke. Abruptly, she found the phone extracted from her fingers, and Jed spoke to her father. The drawl in his voice was more pronounced. His low, cool tone implied that he had the situation under control.

Ana, trembling with reaction, could scarcely believe his arrogance.

'Don't worry, William. No, it's OK. Leave it to me...' he was saying calmly. She shot to her feet, her knees weak with the extent of her fury. Snatching up her clothes, she marched to the bathroom and slammed the door, locking herself in.

Flinging off the robe, she dressed with violent speed. Her only thought was to get out of the hotel room, away from Jed's forceful, un-bearable arrogance. Back at the house, she could ring her father in private. Thrash this out with him, without Jed's dissecting gaze boring into her as she spoke.

The trouble was, when she walked out of the bathroom, Jed would be there. She'd be alone with him again, in his hotel room, and the thought filled her with rising dread. For what seemed an endless stretch of time she sat mo-tionless, on the cork stool by the bath, frozen in a kind of illogical panic. She'd have to face him. There was no way she could stay locked in the bathroom all night. She couldn't jump from a second-floor window...

Rage and fear swirled through her so power-fully, she felt almost dizzy. She was frightened... She tried to clear her head, to work out what she felt most frightened of. Some shadowy kidnap threat she'd only just learned about? Or of Jed Steele, the withdrawn, cynical, manipulative 'professional bodyguard' who was supposedly here to protect her...?

It was too crazy. Too ridiculous. Who in the world would want to kidnap her? An enemy of her father's, the answer shot back straight away. He was rich, he was influential, and he had the power to upset a lot of people as chairman of one of the world's most influential drug companies...

Catching her lip in her teeth, she caught sight of herself in the ornate, gold-framed mirror above the bath. She felt shocked at her appearance. There was a wildness, a savage fury about her slanted brown eyes, her passion-wrecked blonde hair, her full, still swollen lips. How could she still look as if she'd just tumbled out of bed with Jed, when inside she was seething with apprehension, and fear, and uncertainty...?

The episode at Farthingley, four years ago, loomed back into her mind, and she shuddered in memory. Of course, now she knew what Jed had been doing there that weekend. And, because she knew, things made more sense.

He'd been guarding her father. All her gibes about his over-zealous devotion to his job, her frustration at his cold reserve ... She recalled the scene between them on the Sunday, when the conference was over, the high-powered delegates gone. Since the humiliation of Friday night, she'd kept well clear of them all. Made herself scarce with old school friends, picked up briefly on the social life of her childhood. So she'd thought Jed had gone as well. The heatwave had been reaching that stage of humidity unique to hot English summers. Barefoot, wearing only her oversized T-shirt nightdress, she'd been pattering around in the deserted kitchen, long after Ellen had gone to bed, making herself a late supper of tagliatelle. It was one of her favourites. She'd been boiling the pasta, concocting the white wine and mushroom sauce, singing to a Pavarotti tape on her ghetto-blaster, when Jed had appeared inside the door. His soundless entrance had made her jump in fright.

He'd seemed a fraction more relaxed, she recalled now. In fawn chinos and cream denim shirt, he'd seemed less highly charged, slightly more approachable. He'd picked up the wooden spoon she'd dropped on the floor in her fit of nerves, washed it, handed it back, sniffed the aromatic sauce and announced that it was his favourite supper dish as well. After that, once she'd got control of her tendency to blush crimson whenever he looked at her, quenched the shivers of awareness as the green gaze slid coolly over the curves of her body beneath the T-shirt, a relatively relaxed conversation had followed.

She'd got the impression that his effort to be more agreeable was a subtle form of apology for Friday night. So, to show herself to be graciously forgiving, she'd tentatively offered him some of her supper, and when he'd accepted with a wry smile she'd shakily shared it out between two plates. They'd been sitting at the scrubbed elm kitchen table, talking about all kinds of things— opera, acting, her ambitions, liking Italian food, liking travel, liking country picnics and city theatres—when everything had gone black...

Thinking back, his reaction to that had been remarkably rapid, efficient, alert. Far more highly trained than an average person's reaction. He'd appeared to have brilliant night vision, unlike her own, which tended to night-blindness and a ridiculous fear of the dark. Within seconds, he'd located the telephone, rung the local power station via the operator, verified that it was a genuine power cut. He'd found candles and matches, checked upstairs to find that the rest of the household was sound asleep, and then they'd laughingly tried to finish their stone-cold pasta in the eerie, flickering candlelight. The memory of the intimacy of that meal, with the golden halo of candlelight illuminating the hard lines of his face, marooning them together with the deep shadows of the old kitchen all around, was as vivid now as it had been yesterday...

And there'd been a moment, a kind of freeze-frame moment, which had somehow etched itself into her memory, when they'd stopped talking, and the laughter had died away, and the green gaze had held her startled brown one in a long, silent appraisal. Abruptly she'd been conscious of every tiny detail of his appearance, as if someone had pressed the 'pause' button on a video film and she was seeing him in motionless close-up, and as if he was seeing her in exactly the same way...

The atmosphere had altered in some subtle, disturbing way which had sent her heartbeat skittering madly, and hollowed her stomach into an ache of longing...

Jed had broken the spell. His expression had hardened. He'd dropped his eyes to his plate, pushed his fork to the centre, announced it was late, and that he needed to get some sleep. Now that the time had come to go up to bed, she'd hated to show her childish fear of the dark. Steeling herself, she'd put on a fine show of bravado, crept upstairs, forcing herself to ignore the leaping shadows on walls and alcoves. But her candle had blown out in the draught on the landing, drowning her in thick, smothering blackness. Her muffled shriek of distress had brought Jed to investigate, and he'd come into her bedroom and relit the candle.

Amused when he'd guessed her phobia, he'd sat on the edge of her bed, his green gaze narrowed with a mixture of humour, frustration and resignation, and then somehow—she truly couldn't remember how—he'd ended up beside her, his muscular weight disturbingly powerful as he'd moved to pin her there, searched for her mouth. With a groan of despair, he'd kissed her and touched her with a forceful shudder of purpose that she'd found both terrifying and irresistible. All the fleeting arousal of Friday's embrace had been reawakened, but more urgently, more dizzily...

The humiliation of what happened next made her clench her fists now, as she sat rigidly among the jungly luxury of Jed's hotel bathroom. She remembered how he'd guessed, rather than discovered, her inexperience, picked up on her tense, panicky movements, and brought himself ruthlessly back in line.

'Don't you *want* to take my virginity?' she'd whispered, burning with mortification, choked with emotion, and aching, melting, shivering everywhere with bewildered rejection.

'Keep it for someone who matters,' he'd advised shortly, extricating himself from her arms, from her bed, from her room with such cool efficiency that she'd felt wiped out...

Ana drew a deep, shuddering breath. Resolutely she squeezed her eyes tightly shut to blot out the vision of the past. She couldn't sit here all night, racking herself with past failures, reliving the moments of making a cheap fool of herself...

She had to go back out there now; she had to find the strength to face him.

When she finally plucked up courage to emerge, she found Jed sitting comfortably in front of the fire. He'd pulled the black polo-neck back on. The Sunday papers were back in evidence. He was eating a cake and drinking tea. He projected an air of such calm and normality, she felt a fresh wave of confusion. Was she hallucinating? Had the telephone call taken place? Was this how a professional bodyguard behaved when the truth was out, the assignment confirmed...? The sense of unreality deepened.

'I rang for a fresh pot,' he explained coolly as she hovered indecisively between him and the door.

'Don't bother on my account. I can make myself a mug of tea when I get home...'

'Ana...' The authoritarian warning in his voice was the antidote to her uncertainty. She made blindly for the door. With lightning speed, he caught up with her. Her escape was blocked.

'Just calm down,' he advised her cautiously. He was eyeing the flushed heat in her cheeks, the over-bright hysteria in her eyes, with expert assessment. 'You've had a shock. We need to talk about this——'

'I intend to talk to my father about it, *without* your unwelcome presence!' she bit out shakily. 'Get out of my way, Jed!'

'You're not going anywhere,' he informed her, ominously quietly. 'You're going to sit down, calm down, and listen. Right?'

Propelling her in front of him, none too gently, he didn't wait for agreement. He pushed her into a chair beside the tea-table, and eyed her coolly.

There was a short, loaded silence as furious, confused brown eyes clashed with rock-steady green.

'You have every right to be angry,' he said at last, gazing down at her. 'This whole goddamned thing is a fiasco...'

'*Really*?' she managed faintly. 'My father told me you were the *best*. Are you telling me you've messed up your assignment already? Perhaps my father could request a refund?'

His hard mouth tilted with a quirk of humour. 'Don't be a bitch, Ana. It doesn't suit you.'

'You have no idea what suits me!' she told him unsteadily, her voice low and taut with emotion. 'And I don't care what you think of me! It couldn't be any worse than my opinion of *you*——'

'Ana, shut up and listen to me.' His tone was caustic, his eyes scathing as he scanned her flushed face. 'My assignment to protect you is not a fiasco. Our sexual involvement is. I should have foreseen it, and I didn't...'

'No, of course you didn't,' she whispered, icily sarcastic. 'I'm sure you'd forgotten all about our cheap little encounters at Farthingley. As far as you were concerned, nothing happened four years ago, did it? You prowl around like a—an unfeeling robot, you hurt other people's feelings, you destroy other people's dreams, and you don't even *notice*!'

'Ana, could you stop wallowing in self-pity long enough to hear me out!' He sat down opposite her, leaned back in his chair. His eyes were very intent on hers. 'Your father rang me last week. He tracked me down in Rome. He was very worried. An anonymous letter had warned him his daughter was at risk from a terrorist kidnap attack. It was vague, unsubstantiated, and unusual. Kidnappers don't warn their victims in advance. They kidnap someone, then demand a ransom later. So he didn't want to panic you, but he didn't know what the hell to do. He suggested I come to Stratford, keep a distant eye on your movements——'

'He suggested you *spy* on me?' she burst out, aware that she was being unreasonable but too agitated to control her fury. 'Have you had infrared cameras trained on my bedroom window?'

He ignored her.

'However, I judged that the best way of keeping an eye on you was to make contact——'

'And I've made a complete fool of myself, thinking you wanted to...to pick up where we left off? When all the time you're being cold-bloodedly paid to shadow me around? I feel ill, just thinking about this...'

His eyes were intent on her face.

'If I'd told you why I was here, and the threats had proved to be a hoax, I'd have frightened you unnecessarily. But I was concerned about your safety. Even though I hoped there was no danger. I accept I haven't handled this well so far. Like

I said, I misjudged the sexual side. Things got a little out of control, and I didn't plan on that.'

Jed's cool assessment cut like a knife. He'd 'misjudged' this, he 'hadn't planned on that'—the arrogant analysis made her see red.

'I'm overwhelmed by your *kindness* ... !'

'Believe it or not, Ana, in your self-centred temper tantrum, I was thinking of your feelings ...'

Without warning, Jed leaned forward in his chair, and caught her wrists, clamping them in a fierce grip. The colour drained from her face as she met the glitter of cold anger in his gaze.

'Ana, your father had another warning letter this morning. This one had details of your address, your daily movements, your schedule at the theatre, your social habits. Someone is watching you.'

She'd gone very still. Jed's blunt, ruthless statement had finally sunk home.

'Watching me?' she whispered. Her throat was suddenly so dry, she couldn't swallow. The phrase conjured such a dark, shadowy evil, she felt almost physically crushed. Cross with herself for the sweep of pure fear shivering along her spine, she forced a husky laugh. Jed's grip on her wrists had gentled. He still held her, but now the warmth and strength of his fingers was somehow, ironically, reassuring ...

'But ... surely, as you just said, don't kidnappers normally kidnap someone and then send ransom notes? Why would someone watch me and—and then write to my father saying they're *planning* to kidnap me? I don't understand...'

'The key word is "normally",' Jed agreed quietly. 'This character is obviously not normal. Whoever it is we're dealing with is disturbed. They're playing games. Illogical games. In some ways, it's more disconcerting than a "normal" kidnap threat. If any kidnap threat could be described as normal?'

'If they're playing games,' she suggested huskily, freeing her hands to control the tremor of awareness triggered by the warm pressure of his fingers, 'then maybe they're completely harmless, and this is all a—a fuss about nothing? I mean, what motive could they have in compiling all this information about me? Threatening my father like this?'

'Money. That's the usual motive. Or there could be some sort of twisted ideology, or revenge maybe, or professional jealousy involved with your father's pharmaceutical company.'

'Which do *you* think it is?'

'I'm keeping an open mind. That's my job,' he said briefly, sitting back to pour tea into her cup, and passing her the milk. 'The third scenario is that we're dealing with a nutcase. A psychologically disturbed crank. That's the wild card. All we can do is play it by ear, Ana.'

She took a sip of tea, and then restlessly stood up, and stared into the flames of the fire.

'And what, exactly, does that mean?' she demanded softly, turning to see Jed's eyes trained steadily on her. 'Because if it means what I think it means, you can go to hell!'

'It means doing as I tell you,' he agreed wearily, his eyes hardening. 'I guessed you might have a problem with that.'

'I cannot just walk out on my contract with the RSC! I have to fulfil my commitments,' she shot back defensively, 'and if that puts me in the public eye that's just too bad!'

'I need your co-operation, Ana,' he said quietly. 'I can't guarantee to protect you if you don't co-operate.'

'I'll be safe enough on stage, surely? In front of thousands of people? Or maybe you think someone will abseil down from the royal circle, like Tarzan?' she hazarded, with a weak stab at humour.

'I think maybe your father ought to have put you over his knee more often when you were little,' he retorted neutrally.

'If you start claiming I'm spoilt again——'

'You are,' he stated flatly, slowly standing up. 'And when you grow up enough to do something about it, we'll be making some progress.'

'Why, you...' Tension and fury lent strength to the swipe she directed at his head, but the speed with which it was deflected left her pinned against him, spun around with her back to him, her arms locked in a grip of iron, her breathing shallow and erratic.

One strong forearm was crushed across her breasts. The pounding of her heart felt fiercer against the constriction of his arm. She felt her breasts lift and fall beneath the imprisoning hold, and in spite of herself, in spite of him, in spite of everything, a *frisson* of sexual awareness trickled down her spine.

'You think you're so tough and clever,' she whispered shakily. 'I suppose you enjoy demonstrating your *superior* strength whenever you get the chance?'

Jed's reply was a sharp, angry exhalation of breath. As she wriggled defensively against him, he slid his hand across the hardening tips of her breasts, the caress deliberate and controlled. The feel of his warm palm, exploring the swollen studs of her nipples, even through the layer of emerald sweatshirt, made her shudder with need. Her gasp of reaction brought a curt rasp of fury from him.

'And you enjoy demonstrating your sexuality, whenever you get the chance?' he goaded softly. 'Is that it, Ana?'

'You...' Words failed her. A mist of anger blotted out sight and speech. Mutely, she writhed in his grasp. The fight was brief and despicably unequal. She found herself pinioned on his lap as he grimly sat down again, her slender thighs either side of his spread thighs, raw strength trapping her there, her hands locked behind her at the small of her back. The position made her feel helpless, quietly furious, and horribly vulnerable. Her mouth was dry, she couldn't help the awareness of his hard groin beneath hers. If she struggled, the movement brought her sensitised femininity into direct contact with his hard maleness. Even through the modesty of her black leggings, and his denims, it was enough to have a profound effect. Freezing into acquiescence, she saw the dark glitter of mockery in his eyes.

'Stopped fighting?' His deep voice was taunting. He knew, with graphic accuracy, exactly why she'd stopped.

'Let me go,' she whispered. A shudder of distress rocked her, but he didn't relent.

'You know,' he mused with rough humour, 'if it weren't unethical, I'd say the only way to get your co-operation was to take you, make love to you, right now, Ana, whether you say you want it or not.'

Heat rushed to her face. She glared at the stark glint of sexual hunger in his eyes, and her heart began to thud erratically.

'My father is paying you to protect me, not *ravish* me,' she bit out unsteadily, pouring all the scorn she was capable of into her voice, to hide the growing meltdown in her limbs and stomach.

'I know. But if the only way to protect this little shrew is to tame her...?' he taunted. Subtly, he shifted his position beneath her. The unrelenting male challenge made her instinctively clench her muscles. The warm rush of longing felt like liquid fire. Only pride kept her from squirming shamelessly against him...

'I'm not playing Katharina to your Petruchio!' Panic was rising. Her throat had dried, her lips felt parched. She moistened them with her tongue, shivering convulsively.

'No? Aren't you always acting, Ana? Playing Juliet to an invisible Romeo? Spinning some fantasy? Isn't it time reality got a look-in?'

'I hate you...' She whispered the words brokenly. His callous reference to that night in the garden at Farthingley seemed to cut through her anger and defences.

'I don't hate you.' His wry murmur was so deadpan, so ambiguous, she could only gaze at him through tear-blurred eyes.

'No. I know. You're different. I wish I could hurt you as efficiently...'

'Ana...' The green eyes narrowed. The cool brilliance darkened. Cautious emotion swirled in, river-dark, unreadable...

Abruptly she found herself released, swung around, and pushed firmly back on to her chair. His fingers held her shoulders, kneading her tense muscles briefly. His eyes on hers, he smoothed his thumbs slowly through the tears spilling down her cheeks.

'God, Ana, no tears. Don't cry...'

He was still in control of the situation. She couldn't imagine a situation where he wouldn't be in control. But he sounded strangely shaken, she registered dimly. As if an emotional assault had taken him by surprise, where physical and verbal attacks had left him cold...

'What...what do we do now?' she managed to ask.

His mute confirmation of indifference was the worst moment of her life, she realised bleakly. She had to swallow the urge to sob her heart out. Stifle the agony of pain in her stomach. Wasn't that pity she'd detected in his voice?

Among the receding swirl of desire, and the growing pain and misery, she felt empty, cold inside. She dashed the back of her hand impatiently across her wet cheeks.

'We act normally.' Jed spoke abruptly, after a longish pause. He straightened up, sat back in his chair. She was free of his physical restraint. But now she felt so drained, she made no attempt to move.

'How?' She stared at the cup of tea he'd poured her a few minutes earlier. Taking a shaky sip, she struggled to control her thoughts and emotions. With a twist of irony, she recognised that in spite of the implied danger, the invisible threat from some unknown outsider, she'd been talking about the tense situation in the hotel room where they now sat, facing each other, wary as two fighters at the end of a round...

'How can we act normally?' she persisted, gathering strength, collecting her tattered pride.

Passion, infatuation, whatever it was she felt for Jed Steele, had no logic. To shiver convulsively when someone simply reached out a hand and touched you... to crave to get closer to someone who made it clear they wanted you at arm's length? 'This is hardly a *normal* situation, is it?' She mentally tugged herself back in line. She wasn't a trained actress for nothing, was she? If she couldn't portray indifference to match his, she wasn't worth her current contract. 'Or maybe it is a normal situation for you! Of course, you make your living like this, don't you? You "protect" people for money! Let me guess, now you start following me around everywhere, wearing dark glasses and a dark grey suit with a portable phone in the pocket?'

'What the hell are you talking about?' His mouth quirked as he recognised the brave attempt at levity. She wished she could stop watching his mouth. Her stomach hollowed again. Jed's mouth was beautifully shaped, wide, chiselled like a classical sculpture, the lips quite full but hard. The top lip was heavily indented, the lower fractionally asymmetrical. Overall the impression was of controlled sensuality. His half-smile creased deep lines from nose to mouth, cynical, and unreadable. His rare laugh was lopsided and charming and utterly devastating, all at the same time...

'That's how you were dressed when I met you at Farthingley,' she persisted, fighting her idiotic weakness. 'When you were being a "body-guard".'

'I was wearing a suit because it fitted the job,' he pointed out. 'Business executives don't wear Levis.'

'Oh, I see. So the denims fit *this* job?' she concluded, eyeing him with a sudden stab of victory. 'You accuse *me* of role-playing? I'd say we're two of a kind, wouldn't you?'

'Not necessarily.'

The cool rebuttal hurt, but she hardly felt the pain. She was immune to any more humiliation at Jed's hands tonight.

'So what does the *real* Jed Steele wear? When he's not undercover as a business executive or—or a theatre director maybe?'

'Ana, stop trying to compile a neat character sketch of me, will you?' He stood up, flexed broad shoulders, and checked the sleek Rolex on his wrist. 'Let's get back to what we do now. I'll tell you. We go back to your house, collect your things——'

'We do *what*?' Stunned disbelief quickly changed to indignation.

'You heard me.'

'Jed, I'm not collecting my things. I'm not taking my things anywhere. I live there. It's handy for the theatre. I——'

'You still haven't got the message, have you?' The rasp of harsh authority to his deep voice brought her to a halt. He swung round, his eyes coolly intent on her white face. 'I've seen your house. I can't guarantee protection there. It's too casual. Too open to unwelcome visitors. If you're determined to stick it out at the theatre, Ana, you'll move your stuff in here for now. Where I can keep an eye on you. And that,' he finished up, ominous slivers of ice in his green gaze, 'is not negotiable.'

CHAPTER FIVE

FEELING grateful to Jed Steele was a humbling experience, Ana decided bleakly, running the gauntlet of teasing and gibes as she left the theatre a week later.

It was also deeply ironic. He might be a secret source of reassurance, when she let herself dwell on the horrors of the kidnap threat. But a week had gone by. A whole week. No one had tried to grab her and bundle her into the back of a lorry. No one had pounced on her backstage and pushed a sack over her head...

She was beginning to think the whole charade was ridiculous. And he might have demonstrated some consideration for her needs—hadn't he overridden her father's insistence that she drop her acting career and come running home to Farthingley?—but having him around her all the time was driving her slowly crazy... out of her mind with frustration and humiliation and confusion...

It was affecting her acting, she felt sure of it. Having Jed sleeping in the next room, having him watch over her with that implacable, impassive scrutiny—she'd never felt more insecure about her own femininity, never felt so self-conscious and awkward in her whole life.

And on top of all that his very *presence* in her life at the theatre was causing her more embarrassment than she'd ever imagined possible...

''Night, Ana,' Camilla trilled, grinning, exchanging glances with Pru, as Ana swiftly scanned her pigeon-hole at the stage door. 'Sleep well. That's if you *get* any sleep, darling, being "bodyguarded" all night long.'

'Thanks, Camilla,' Ana murmured drily. Absently, she extracted a couple of letters from the rack, and turned to see her friend slanting her eyes at Jed with sensual deliberation.

Ana's heart jerked. Jed, dispassionately scanning the comings and goings of the stage door, lean and self-contained and ever watchful, looked devastatingly attractive. No wonder Camilla, and most of the other actresses in the company for that matter, looked at him the way Camilla was looking at him now...

She caught his eye, and received a faint lift of his eyebrow in response to her nervous smile. He was lounging with cool composure against the wall, waiting for her. Casual in high-necked white cotton shirt, brown leather waistcoat, butter-coloured suede bomber-jacket, Levis and brown leather boots, his appearance blended well with the relaxed, verging on scruffy style beloved of the cast and crew. But his style had a cosmopolitan air. Something, Ana reflected reluctantly, something about him, whether it was the cut or fabric or shape of his clothes, or that mask-like control of his features—something marked him down as someone of influence, someone with authority—and someone, she reminded herself bitterly, with a great deal of money earned through the manipulation of other people's fears...

'You know, I think you should let your hunky bodyguard *inside* our dressing-room on Monday,' Camilla persisted, following them out of the door into the cool night air, and watching Ana hug her velvet jacket around herself with a shiver of self-protection. '*My* body feels like it needs guarding!'

'The only thing you have that needs guarding is your tongue,' Jed quipped briefly. The cool sarcasm and the deadpan delivery combined effectively to silence Camilla. In spite of herself, as she watched her friend flounce out of sight, Ana found it hard to suppress a twinge of amusement.

'You were hard on Camilla,' she said as they rounded the corner and stopped by the car. The big, gunmetal-grey BMW 7 series was parked in the theatre's 'No Parking' access road, to the impotent fury of Arthur at the stage door reception desk. Taunting grins and witty gibes were all she heard as the cast and crew filed past on their way home, while Jed conducted his rapid check of the vehicle.

'That's not how I'd describe it.' Jed glanced across the width of the bonnet, straightening up and unlocking the doors. 'OK, get in.'

'Yes, *sir*.' How much longer could she stand this? Being ordered about, shepherded around, treated like a half-wit? Mocked mercilessly by everyone at the theatre?

They were in the car, reversing out into the road, through the crowds of theatre-goers making their way towards the pubs and restaurants of Stratford.

'You're used to demolishing people,' she returned to the attack, 'so you wouldn't even notice if you were being hard on someone.'

'That's an unfair criticism. I'm trained to protect people.' He wrenched the steering-wheel around, swerving to avoid a group of youths running across the road, and she had to suppress the urge to scream. He was glancing in the driving mirror, presumably at the young men they'd just missed. His expression was cool, thoughtful, and insultingly uninterested in what she had to say to him.

'Camilla is a friend of mine. She was only being facetious.'

'I'll make a point of being kinder to her in future.' There was an ominous edge to his voice that she couldn't interpret.

'Maybe you should bear in mind that you're being paid to be kind to *me*.'

'I'm being paid to keep you safe.' Jed glanced obliquely at her as they drove into the car park of the hotel. 'Kindness doesn't come into it.'

'Come to think of it, maybe I'm more in need of protection from *you* than from this mystery crank?'

'I doubt that.'

She shot him a wary look as they arrived at the suite of rooms he'd organised. She had her own bedroom and *en-suite* bathroom, but it still felt agonisingly intimate. The familiar, sinking sensation was beginning in her stomach, the way it did every time she walked in here, knowing she'd be spending the night within a few feet of Jed...

'Why *are* you doing all this, Jed?' she said slowly, following him inside and observing the professional, lightning check of the rooms, windows, wardrobes, beds.

'Standard procedure.' He grinned briefly over his shoulder.

'No, I mean, why agree to protect me?'

'Your father asked me to.'

'I know he did. But you could have said no. You could have recommended someone else.'

'The money's good.' His tone was sardonic.

Flicking him a withering glance, she walked stiffly into her bedroom, tossed her jacket on to a chair, and slammed the door against him. Her throat was dry with nerves. She toyed with the rebellious idea of locking the door, and after a moment's hesitation defiantly shot the bolt. The connecting door was to stay unlocked, Jed's orders had been. To hell with him tonight... She marched into the bathroom, shrugged off her jeans and floppy blue jumper, and stepped under a reviving hot shower.

Surely, soon, she'd begin to acquire a degree of immunity to Jed's constant nearness? His contained lack of interest should be gradually lulling her into a sense of security, shouldn't it? Blinking at her pale reflection in the mirror, as she dried herself and scrubbed her teeth, she conceded that that was a faint hope. She'd only be immune to Jed Steele if she were dead...

He hadn't touched her all week. The ease with which he'd switched from that sensual assault a week ago to this—this inhuman restraint was deeply insulting.

She stared at herself in the mirror, furious at her crazy thoughts. What was she thinking? It wasn't that she *wanted* him to touch her! The prospect of her own weakness terrified her...

But, illogically, this cold-blooded single-mindedness made her want to lash out at him.

She enveloped herself in the gold towelling bathrobe supplied by the hotel, and emerged. Her jacket still lay on the chair where she'd thrown it. Making a conscious effort at tidiness, she picked it up, with the noble intention of hanging it up in the wardrobe. The letters she'd collected from her pigeon-hole were sticking out of the pocket.

She snatched them out, dropped the jacket on the floor, sat down on the chair, opened the first one, and began to read. Her vision blurred and danced. Panic overtook her. She gave a choked cry, and dropped the paper to the floor as if it had burned her.

'Ana?' Jed's deep voice was clipped as he found the door locked. 'Ana, what is it? Open the door.'

She stared at the letter, not focusing on it. She felt frozen to the chair, unable to move.

'Ana? Ana, open this door, *now*!' Jed's voice held such an icy imperative that she pulled herself together and staggered to unbolt it. He flung the door wide and strode in, controlled fury in every line of his body.

'What the hell are you playing at? I said don't lock the door.'

Her fingers trembling, she pointed to the piece of plain white A4 paper, lying beside her velvet jacket on the floor. Jed crouched to retrieve it, slowly straightening up as he studied it. The words, instead of being typed or cut out of magazines in the time-honoured fashion, had been printed on a Dymo-tape machine and stuck on in thin block strips.

'"Think you're safe?"' he read aloud. '"Watch this space..."'

He turned his narrow gaze on her. She ran her tongue shakily around her dry lips. This sense of intimidation was out of all proportion to the threat, she told herself furiously. But she couldn't help it. She was shuddering inside...

'No great literary genius,' Jed remarked, glancing at her colourless face and huge dark eyes with a gleam of reassuring humour. 'And if it's like the others sent to your father, there may be some more traceable clues. Where's the envelope? I'll get someone from my company to check it out, Ana.'

'Your...company?' Stiffly, she retrieved the envelope from the floor. It had been hand-delivered. Maybe that, more than the message itself, was what had sent the cold trickle of fear down her spine.

'Worldwide Security,' he supplied shortly, meeting her confused gaze impassively.

'I—I thought you operated alone.' She was being led, firmly but gently, towards her bed.

'I used to. Not any more. Get into bed, Ana. I'll order you some tea.'

Her passion for tea hadn't escaped him, she reflected dimly. She was being idiotic, shaking like a leaf, when all she'd done was open and read an anonymous letter...

'Jed, this is scary,' she whispered. 'Some-how...the thought of someone putting that letter there, by hand, having the nerve to come into the theatre to—to leave it for me...'

'Sure it's scary. That's why I'm here. Remember?'

'Yes . . .' She met the rare smile, the one which almost reached his eyes, the one that curved two lean furrows from nose to mouth. Her heart stopped shrinking in fear. Instead it seemed to swell with foolish emotion.

Glad of the demure folds of the gold bathrobe, she climbed into bed, and lay weakly back against the pillows. She realised how exhausted she felt. Performing on stage, even in her small non-speaking part in tonight's play, was a gruelling three-hour stint. And by Saturday night, after a full week of nightly performances and two matinées, she was utterly pole-axed. On top of everything else, this extra stress felt unbearable...

She was almost asleep when Jed came back with a tray of tea. Opening her eyes sleepily, she saw him standing by the bed, looking down at her. His expression was unfathomable.

'I've spoken to your father,' he said, handing her a cup, and taking one for himself. He sat on the small, button-backed chair by the bed, and watched her steadily. 'There's only a couple of nights left before your ten-day break, Ana. I'm not prepared to take the risk. I'm taking you out of here tomorrow.'

Her fingers clenched on the cup. Wriggling to sit up properly, she almost spilled the hot tea.

'Jed,' she began in a low, shaky voice, 'I can't go anywhere; I'm committed to appear in three plays and——'

'Look at yourself, Ana,' he cut in. He sounded implacable. Arguing, she sensed wearily, was going to be like hitting her head against a stone wall. 'You're exhausted. You'll get ill if you don't stop pushing yourself. We'll get through this, then you can get back to your career. Right now your safety is more important.'

'You can't make me go anywhere,' she shot back unsteadily, 'unless *you're* proposing to kidnap me?'

'Call it what you like. The flight leaves tomorrow morning, early. We'll be on it.'

She felt heat flood her whole body, then vanish again, leaving her cold, shivery and tense with a combination of anger and fear.

'I will *not*...' she started to say, her voice rising to border on hysteria. Swinging her legs out of bed, she made to lunge past Jed, caught her foot in the hem of the bathrobe, and catapulted ignominiously into his arms. Catching her easily, he steadied her against him, then held her away a fraction, examining his wriggling victim.

'If I have to lock you in your bedroom tonight, I will,' he told her coolly. 'If I don't get you out of here, I wouldn't be fulfilling my promise to your father...'

Wildly, she glared at the darkly impassive face. The blood was thundering through her veins, and she wasn't sure if it was fury or a more subtle, insidious reaction to his touch.

'Jed, don't bully me into this,' she whispered, a shiver of awareness feathering her spine. What was wrong with her? This sexual force between them wasn't the important issue right now—she was trying to maintain her independence, assert her right to decide... So why wasn't she fighting her feelings? A week ago, her defences had rescued her. Pride, inexperience, the horror of Jed finding out about the lasting impression he'd made on her life...

But now... now it was beginning all over again—was it the hard warmth of his body, the intimate contact after the week of abstinence, that was wreaking havoc with her emotions?

'Don't force me to bully you into it,' he countered calmly. But there was a darker gleam in his eyes. A pulse jerked erratically at his jawline.

Ana stared into his eyes. Fragments of the past seemed to swirl into the present. The night in the garden at Farthingley, the way she'd felt as he'd challenged her about her perfume, when she'd stepped closer with innocent seduction... the night in her room, when he'd reassured her about the power cut, discovered she was terrified of the dark, and one thing had almost led to another...

'Jed...' She heard herself whisper his name huskily, a throaty moan which sounded like someone else's voice. Blindly, she moved closer, so that her breasts were pressed against his chest.

He'd abandoned the waistcoat and suede jacket. He felt reassuringly hard and strong and warm through the white cotton shirt. But no, not reassuring. Unnerving ... disturbing ... Her senses kaleidoscoped. Without thinking, her fingers pushed up, across the width of male shoulders braced to support her weight, and into the crisp spring of clean, shiny brown hair. She closed her eyes, and saw darkly swirling colours behind her eyelids. It was a sensual delight, both forbidden and thrilling. The unspoken restraint between them since last weekend was being bridged by her own daring, and she had no idea if she was proud or ashamed of herself. She wasn't thinking straight enough to tell either way—her senses were blurring into some primitive, brain-numbing world of their own...

'Ana...' Jed's voice sounded rough, fractionally strangled. His hands tightened at her waist, as if to push her away. Letting her fingers move of their own volition, she cupped his head in her hands, stroked the lean contours of his face, explored the smooth, taut, tanned skin down to where the shadow of beard-growth coarsened his jawline.

'Please ... I have to stay in Stratford until Wednesday, Jed...' she murmured huskily, hardly knowing what she was doing as she caressed the strong column of his neck. 'I—I'll make it worth your while...'

Had she actually *said* that? An appalled shiver went through her. But with trembling fingers she undid the top button of the high-necked shirt, then another button, and another. The iron-firm muscle of his chest, whorled with a patch of dark, coarse hair between flat, tight nipples, was revealed to her view, and she felt her throat dry so much that she doubted if she could speak any more...

'You conniving little bitch,' he grated softly, not moving to stop her. A shudder went through him. His narrowed eyes were brilliant with the glitter of mockery, but the pupils were dilated, his gaze sliding over her unfathomably.

'Don't you want to—to make love to me any more?' Just as she'd feared, her voice was cracking, letting her down. Her mouth felt like sandpaper. Her heart pounded so fast, she felt faint.

'As part of a bribe to get your own way?' he taunted quietly. But his voice shook. A pulse was beating hard at his throat. Closing her eyes, she opened her mouth and instinctively let her lips trail over his chest. Her head was whirling. *Was* she doing this to get her own way? She hadn't the least idea what her real motive was. Now she knew what it was like to be blinded by desire. To be on fire for one particular person, no matter what they felt about her, no matter what past experience had taught her—she should stop this, stop it now—it was madness. She was humili-

ating herself all over again. Part of her brain
dutifully registered this information. But now
she'd come this far, for the life of her she couldn't
seem to stop herself. It was like dying of thirst
and being offered a punch-bowl brimming with
crystal-clear water...

'Jed, please...'

'I don't believe this,' he murmured huskily,
levering her away and raking her trembling body
with his eyes. He sounded part angry, part
amused, part shaken by a desire he'd rather deny.
'You're officially my client now, Ana. I avoid
emotional involvement with my clients. Besides,
is this the same Ana who told me to get the hell
out of her life a week ago?'

'Jed...'

'And you'd sacrifice your aversion to me, for
the sake of your career?' he mocked bleakly.

'I...' The gold robe had fallen open, she registered belatedly. She was standing close to him,
and her body was exposed to his interested, lazy
inspection. Where his eyes moved, her flesh responded involuntarily. The small swell of her
breasts tingled. The nipples pulled tight, crunched
into hard little buttons of desire. Her stomach
hollowed. A warm heat dissolved between her
thighs.

She blinked at him. What was she doing? It
might, fleetingly, have started as a notion to sway
his decision. But now it was the unleashing of
that tightly suppressed longing. She was back in

Farthingley, before his cruel rejection. She was shaking so violently, she might have a fever...

'Make love to me, Jed,' she choked in a low sob. 'Now. Please...?'

'*Jeez*...sweet hell, Ana...' His fingers bit deep into her arms as he roughly shoved her off. 'You seriously think I'd fall for this routine?'

'Routine?' she whispered fiercely. 'Is that what you think it is? Maybe you think this is something I do all the time? This...this talk about emotional involvement with your clients—you just avoid emotional involvement, period. Don't you?'

'It keeps life a lot tidier.'

'You really know how to twist the knife, don't you?'

'I know when to pull out of a situation, sweetheart,' he mocked hoarsely, his voice so thick with desire, it was unrecognisable. 'You have a beautiful body. I want you like crazy. I don't like being manipulated. Forget the seduction. Go to sleep.'

Without a backward glance, he turned and strode out, extracting the key from the door and locking it from the other side. Scarcely able to register his arrogant rejection, she threw herself down on the bed. Trapped, made a fool of a third time, rejected a third time...locked in her *room*, like a naughty child? She might as well be kidnapped by her unknown enemy, she reflected with bitter passion. In an orgy of temper and pain,

she clutched the pillow over her head while she
sobbed with the fiercest fury she'd ever felt in
her life...

It was a grey, still morning as they drove down
the M40 to Heathrow.

'I feel as if I should be handcuffed to you, like
a prisoner in transit,' she informed Jed at the
airport, a hectic glitter in her eyes as she met his.
They'd been through the check-in procedures and
only now could she manage to control her blind
fury sufficiently to ask where they were going.

'Antigua,' Jed informed her. He was scanning
the other passengers in the first-class lounge, his
gaze coolly watchful. In cool fawn chinos, white
polo-shirt, with the butter-coloured suede jacket
over his shoulders, he looked elegant, and horribly well-rested. How could he look so relaxed
and healthy, when she looked as if she'd been ten
rounds with Mohammed Ali?

What would he do if someone rushed up to her
and tried to kidnap her? she wondered wildly.
Pull a gun? Did he *carry* a gun? She'd never asked
him. Never noticed if he did...

'*Antigua*? Oh, wow. Am I supposed to be im-
pressed?' she snapped. She needed some dark
glasses, to hide her puffy, sleep-deprived eyes.
She was aware that she was behaving appallingly,
but she was so angry, so exhausted, so wound
up, she couldn't help it. Thrusting her hands hard

into the pockets of her jacket, she stared at the carpeted floor, hating him and herself...

He didn't bother to reply. She drew her hands out of her pockets and hugged them around herself miserably. Last night still hurt like a knife in her solar plexus. At least she'd emerged from the sad little fiasco with a shred of credibility. It was better to let him believe she'd been trying to manipulate him into letting her stay in Stratford, wasn't it? Less humiliating than admitting she'd been drowning, all over again, in that familiar, destructive flashflood of desire...

'Am I allowed to go to the Ladies unaccompanied?' she demanded, when he appeared to be all set to ignore her for the duration.

'Sure. Be my guest.'

In spite of her defiance, she felt uneasy locking herself into one of the cubicles. Her nerves were so frayed, she was jumpy, irrational. The end cubicle was occupied when she came out of hers, and the notion that someone could be lurking in there, waiting to pounce out on her, was so idiotic that she felt furious with herself as she splashed cold water on her red eyes, and blew her nose hard on a tissue. She'd spent the most awful night, tossing and turning, sleeping only fitfully, and, when she slept, dreaming disjointed, tormenting snatches of dreams, all of which seemed to feature that long-ago night in her bedroom at Farthingley, and Jed's cavalier reaction to discovering her nineteen-year-old virginity...

How had she lost her head last night sufficiently to repeat the whole humiliating process? Had it been reaction to opening that letter? The adrenalin, triggered by her first taste of real, stomach-churning fear? Whatever the excuse, it was beyond belief, she thought, hating her reflection, despising herself fiercely. In floppy tan cotton jacket, white T-shirt and black cotton trousers, her blonde hair piled up into a haphazard topknot, with strands escaping wildly in all directions, she looked just as she felt. Dishevelled, exhausted, thoroughly unappealing. She was frowning at herself in the mirror with such bleak distaste that she received an alarmed look from the very normal-looking woman who emerged from the end cubicle to wash her hands...

She didn't normally sleep on air journeys. But the endless flight to Antigua came on top of her restless night, and she fell into a dead sleep, waking to find her head pillowed on Jed's hard suede shoulder. She jerked up and almost cricked her neck in her haste to put distance between them. For the rest of the flight, punctuated by meals and drinks, she alternately dozed, watched the in-flight movies including an idiotic romp with Goldie Hawn, and read a romantic thriller she'd bought at the airport. She was glad she'd bought dark glasses along with the book. They gave her the privacy she needed, while she licked

her wounded pride. Jed read a slim psycho-
logical suspense novel, written by Brian Moore,
the Irish writer who he informed her briefly was
a favourite of his.

The time-difference meant that it was still only
mid-afternoon when they finally circled to land.

'I hope all this is worth it,' she muttered, too
tense to admit the small surge of excitement she
was feeling, watching the brilliant green hump of
the island loom up beneath them, coral-ringed in
a sapphire sea. 'Who else knows we've come
here?'

'No one. Your father knows roughly where we
are——' Jed raised a cool eyebrow at her continuing mutiny '—but I haven't told him exactly
where. I've given him a contact in Miami. I have
an office there. He can get in touch when
necessary.'

'You don't trust my father?'

'Of course I trust your father. But the fewer
people who know the better. I can't rule out the
possibility that this kidnap threat could be
coming from someone within the company.'

She flipped off the dark glasses then, staring
at him in surprise.

'Are you serious? You think someone my
father employs would do something like issue
kidnap threats?'

'Not necessarily. I have a couple of theories.
My people are working on them. All you have to
do is relax here, Ana. Forget your problems.'

Relax? With Jed in close proximity? She'd sooner try and relax on a bed of nails...

But even the air of the airport smelled seductive as she stepped off the small plane. The airport shimmered in the Caribbean warmth. Ranks of tall palms tossed their green heads languidly in the offshore breeze. As they'd landed she'd glimpsed sugar-white coves, backed by jungly green, facing the endless blue of the ocean. The contrast to the misty cool of England was so intense, she held on to her composure with difficulty...

There was a man striding towards them as they completed the formalities in the airport and emerged with their luggage. He was slim and deeply tanned, in Levis and casual shirt. His short, thick brown hair was roughly the colour of Jed's, but tinged with grey at the temples.

'Jed! Hey, how are you?' There was a warm hand-clasp, then a very American-style bear-hug.

'OK. Good, in fact. How about you?'

'Great. Can't complain...' The man was slightly shorter than Jed, and around ten years older. He turned curious blue eyes on Ana, who found herself responding to his friendly smile, despite her defiant resolution to stay aloof throughout her enforced stay.

'Ana, this is a friend of mine, Blake Sheraton.'

'How do you do?' Her stomach clenched in wry astonishment as she politely shook hands. A friend? Jed Steele was human enough to have a *friend*?

'Blake and his wife Nina came over here from Florida a couple of years ago. They run a hotel on the island.'

'Great to meet you, Ana. Nina's in a high state of excitement. She can't wait to meet a real-life actress with the Royal Shakespeare Company...'

'No time to waste, then,' Ana heard herself reply coolly, avoiding Jed's hard glance. 'Since I was forced to run out on my contract last night, I doubt if I'll be one for much longer!'

On the bumpy drive through the island, Ana sat in the back in silence. Jed and Blake, having exchanged a brief, telling glance, sat in front, and talked sporadically. She stared resentfully at the back of Jed's dark head, at the thickness of his hair, the powerful slope of his shoulders. His hair brushed the top of his collar, waving slightly into a point at the sensuously golden skin of his nape. She remembered how she'd touched his neck last night, and a deep, silent shudder of awareness ran right through her, from her breasts to her thighs...

Jed and Blake were laughing about something. Their easy conversation was open enough to reveal a friendship of long standing. It became apparent that Blake had once inhabited the same tough world as Jed. And that Jed spent a lot of time out here, relaxing between jobs.

She felt utterly confused. She wished she hadn't been rude. She wished she could work out how she felt. Somehow, while she felt sure that she was perfectly entitled to feel angry, and bullied, and patronised, she felt as if the ground had been swept from under her feet. While the Jeep racketed between palm trees, looped down to skirt dazzling white beaches, plunged back into greenery again, she searched her mind for the answer to her fresh confusion...

With a jolt, she identified it. Like it or not, another set of emotions was overriding her mutinous defiance, her damaged pride, her trampled ego, eclipsing even the lurking fear of the threats to her safety.

She was being given a brief, unexpected glimpse into the private life of the most private man she'd ever met...

For the first time since she'd known Jed, she was getting the chance to discover something about him, maybe even get to know the real man behind the barricades. And she had no idea how she was going to handle the situation...

CHAPTER SIX

'SO HOW'S the theatre coping without you?' Nina asked, eyeing Ana with her wide, friendly hazel gaze. 'Doesn't the entire programme fall apart if one of the actors goes missing?'

'Not exactly,' Ana admitted. 'There's a complicated system of understudies...' She made a determined effort to smile at Blake's pretty, dark-haired wife across the dinner-table, now littered with the remains of an exquisite meal of fruit, fish, salads and exotic vegetables. Candlelight flickered in a glass shade, making a pinkish glow on the cream damask cloth, flickering darts of flame in the brilliance of the silverware, the glitter of lead crystal.

The setting, in the thatch-shaded open-air beach restaurant of the hotel, was sumptuously luxurious. Velvet dark palms and cascades of fluorescent-bright tropical flowers billowed in every direction. White-jacketed waiters skimmed through the tables, well-heeled guests conducted low-voiced, highly bred dinner conversation. Just beyond the terrace, the ocean sucked and crashed on to the beach. A warm wind rustled the dry palm leaves.

The guests seemed to include several different nationalities, but Ana wryly guessed that they all shared two things in common: vast wealth and impeccable breeding. She recognised these types of people. Her father's wealth had meant that she'd mixed in circles like these. But something in her had always rebelled against ostentation or pretentiousness.

Occasionally, amid the clink of glasses and the chink of fine porcelain, there was the pop of a champagne cork, a peal of modulated laughter. But overall the atmosphere was so refined that the actress in her almost felt a perverse urge to jump on to the table and belt out a raunchy pop song, with appropriate gyrations to match...

She restrained herself. Clearly Blake and Nina ran a highly profitable, exclusive set-up. Blake had been proudly describing the facilities. Everything seemed to be on offer, from free scuba-diving to tennis, a choice of three beaches, a boutique selling souvenirs and beachwear, nearly forty acres of tropical grounds to wander in at will...

They'd given her and Jed what they called 'beach-front' cottages—small thatched affairs only a few feet above the high-tide line, with balconies overlooking the most romantic sunset Ana had ever seen. 'Expect a few downpours,' Blake had grinned. 'It is the rainy season. But rain doesn't last long here. And Antigua's the driest of the Leeward Islands. So just relax...'

As they were sitting in the balmy evening air, with the hypnotic whirr of the cicadas as continuous background music, it was hard not to begin to relax.

Jed's presence on the other side of the table, broodingly attractive in forest-green silk shirt and smoke-grey cotton suit, was annihilating her composure, but that was nothing new. At least Blake and Nina were reassuringly normal, talkative, confiding, and curious. In their early forties, they projected a positive energy which would probably keep them young forever. She found herself liking them very much.

'So if an actor gets sick, there's always someone to step in and fill the gap?' Nina was saying, her eyes fascinated.

Ana nodded, toying with the long stem of her wine glass.

'Yes. For instance, I'm in three plays. I've got a small, reasonable speaking part in one, non-speaking crowd scene parts in the other two, but I'm understudying the main female role in one of those plays. So if someone's ill...'

'But you're not ill,' Nina finished up, with a glimmer of sympathy in her smile, 'and you're worried about letting everyone down.'

'Yes.'

'*And* you're worried about these kidnap threats,' Nina reminded her. 'Aren't you?'

'Yes.'

'You poor kid,' Blake laughed, not unkindly, flexing his shoulders and pouring some more wine into her glass. 'Make the most of your holiday here. You look like you need one!'

'Given my current predicament, I don't really have any choice, do I?'

'No, you don't.' Jed's interjection was coolly expressionless. 'So how about dropping the martyred performance, and admitting you're enjoying yourself already?'

Ana felt a flush warm her cheeks. Turning slowly, she met Jed's hard green gaze, and felt it slide mockingly over her bare shoulders, skim down across the brilliant pink silk of her short, strapless evening dress, linger with blatant interest on the pale swell of her breasts beneath the bodice.

'Oh, I *am*,' she flashed back, a bright flash of hostility in her dark eyes. 'I'm having a *wonderful* time, thank you. In fact, why don't you drop your stiff-necked *bodyguard* performance, and come and dance with me, Jed?'

'I don't dance.' Jed's face was granite-hard, his eyes ominously narrowed.

Nina and Blake were exchanging amused looks.

'But I want to dance,' Ana persisted, adopting her most spoiled-brat voice. 'And what if someone tries to grab me on the dance-floor? I'm sure my father is paying you enough to humour your *client*?'

With a tilted eyebrow at Blake, Jed slowly rose to his feet. The music, played by a live band at the far side of the terrace beneath some floodlit palms, was an alluring Caribbean blend of steel band and saxophone, the beat intensely primitive and arousing. In spite of their undoubted gentility, several couples were already moving about the small, intimate dance-floor, with varying degrees of sensuality, entwined together, their relationship clear for all to see.

'I'd better ensure the client gets value for money,' Jed murmured laconically, cupping her elbow to guide her through the tables, his fingers far from gentle against her bare flesh.

Some imp of angry mischief had seized her, prompted by the insidious shivers of reaction to his touch. Reaching a clear space, just as the tempo of the music speeded up, she spun into Jed's arms, and began to move in a deliberately inflammatory way against him.

'What kind of a dance is this?' he enquired smokily, catching her round the waist, a dangerous softness in his voice.

'Didn't you ever see *Dirty Dancing*?' she goaded softly. With an abandon she'd never known she possessed, she let her fingers cling with feminine suggestiveness to the breadth of his shoulders, let her hips arch sensuously forward into his, swaying with all the provocation of a professional stripper. There was a hectic brilliance in her eyes. Her face, in fact her whole body, felt feverishly heated. Deep inside, in the hollow of her stomach, was a pain, a clenched anticipation of rejection. But her fury at his snide treatment of her, her urge to hit back spurred her on blindly...

'Yeah, I saw it,' he growled huskily, his eyes dropping to the thrust of her small breasts inside her dress, to the points of her nipples, straining beneath the silk. 'But you're out of luck. I didn't go to the same dance school as Patrick Swayze.'

'You didn't?' she shot back recklessly. 'Never mind, I trained in dance as well as acting. I'll teach you...'

'You'll teach me?' he warned harshly, crushing her against the hard length of him, almost knocking her breath away. 'I doubt it, Ana. The problem is, you never learn, sweetheart...'

She started to retort, but one lean hand snaked around the nape of her neck, beneath the heavy, glossy curtain of blonde hair, and the other clamped her hips to his. Their pretence of dancing was abruptly over. Instead Ana found herself being kissed with a ferocious force which took her wholly by surprise, took no account of her vulnerability, made not even the faintest pretence of respecting her, as a woman...

Jed ravished the softness of her lips, his tongue plunging inside the dark cavity of her mouth, with openly mocking sexuality. With masculine strength, he ground her so intimately to the steely length of his body that she felt as if he was taking her, making love to her, right there in the middle of the dance-floor. She could feel the powerful ripple of muscle in his back as she clung to him. She could feel, to her mounting chagrin, the unmistakable bulge of his arousal, hard against the softness of her stomach...

When he released her, abruptly, angrily, she almost fell. She felt as if her thighs had vanished. Grasping at his shoulders, she managed to stop herself from collapsing. She could taste a trace of blood on her lower lip. Her pulses were juddering, her head felt light and dizzy.

'Come on,' he snapped, jerking her off the dance-floor and away from the interested audience they'd begun to attract. Plunging into the humid, cicada-filled darkness, she found herself frogmarched down to the beach. The coral sand crunched beneath her sandals.

Half furious, half sobbing, she rounded on him as they reached the water's edge.

'What's the matter with you?' she choked, shivering despite the warmth of the night. 'You're supposed to be protecting me, not—not assaulting me...!'

Jed had let go of her, and was standing, breathing slightly erratically, a few feet away. His profile was forbidding.

'I know,' he agreed finally. His voice held a rough note which was new to her. He sounded roughly furious, but with himself. 'I'm sorry. I shouldn't let you provoke me. God knows, I've had enough experience of it...'

She controlled her ragged breathing. Sinking down on to the still warm sand, she kicked off her high-heeled sandals, hugged her arms round her bare knees. The smell of the ocean was clean, pure, exhilarating. She tried to inhale it to the very bottom of her lungs, to rid herself of this sense of shame, of self-disgust...

'You mean...with me?' she asked shakily.

Jed sat down too, a few feet away. He didn't look at her.

'Yes. With you...'

'Do you hate me so much?' It was painful to ask. But Ana felt as if her whole world had shrunk to this moment, this tense little scene on a tropical beach. Nothing else mattered but the truth...

'I don't hate you.'

'Then what do you feel?'

Jed turned slowly to look at her. There was a huge moon, suspended in the dark sky like a rosy-gold pumpkin. Its light strode a pale path over the vastness of the ocean to carve harsh shadows beneath his gaunt cheekbones. His gaze was devastatingly cool and steady on her white face.

'Right now? A sense of duty,' he said shortly.

'No, not right now,' she blurted out, goaded past caring. 'Any time. What have you *ever* felt for me, Jed? Apart from pity, maybe.'

'*Pity*?' he echoed sharply. 'Why the hell should I pity you—the spoiled little rich girl with everything, used to instant admiration from every male in a ten-mile radius?'

'That's what you *always* say to me!' she exploded, balling her fists in frustration. 'Do you think I'd have all this—this ambition to succeed on my own if I were your "spoiled little rich girl"? Do you think I'd have worked my way through the last two years of drama school, refusing my father's help, if I were spoiled...?'

She bit her lip. What had made her blurt that out?

Jed's gaze raked her with suppressed curiosity.

'You did that?' He assessed the information in detached, faintly amused silence. 'How about the first year?'

I hadn't met you then, she retorted silently, staring at him in mounting indignation. I hadn't been made to feel guilty about having a rich father. I hadn't met the man I felt compelled to prove something to...

'You've always sneered at me,' she countered huskily, 'but are you so damned perfect? Jared Steel, Superman? No faults or vices?'

'No.' His clipped retort sounded huskier, too. He was sitting on the sand, only a few feet away from her. But the tension between them electrified the darkness.

'No? You mean you admit to some failings?' she mocked.

'I've failed people in my life.'

'Who?' she demanded softly, sensing some change in him, but not quite sure what. 'Who have you failed, Jed?'

There was a taut silence. Then Jed said expressionlessly, 'My mother, for one, when she died, and I couldn't save her...'

Ana caught her breath. Turning to look at the rigid profile beside her, she felt a pain twist in her chest. Tears filled her eyes. Jed's pain was so unexpected, so raw, for all his cool lack of emotion, that it hit her with a force which wiped out her defences. For a long moment, she could think of nothing to say. Her throat felt too dry for words. Moistening her lips with her tongue, she finally said carefully, unsteadily, 'You *failed* her? Jed, I don't think you believe that for one moment, do you? *Do* you? Or are you saying that you deliberately caused whatever accident happened?'

'No...*no*...' His response was rough with impatient emotion.

'But you feel guilt? For things that weren't your fault?'

'Maybe.' The curt response signalled a termination of the conversation. He started to get up, and she rose to her knees, grabbed his arm, held him still. She could hardly see him through the mist of tears. She clung to him urgently, felt him go very still as she pulled him back.

'Will you talk to me? Tell me what happened?'

'It happened a long time ago. I don't want to discuss it now...'

'Is that why you do what you do? Guard people? Protect them for a living? To make up for what happened? To—to try to compensate?'

'Don't try to psychoanalyse me, Ana.' He spoke with a trace of bleak amusement. 'You're over-reacting again. I'm not crazy. I know what happened wasn't directly my fault. Rationally, I know that. That doesn't stop the sense of failure. It may not make sense, but I can live with that...'

'But that kind of stupid, unfounded guilt can—can eat away at you,' she reasoned in a more controlled voice. She dashed a hand over her eyes, willing herself to stay in control, when all she really wanted to do was cradle him in her arms, hold him so tightly that he'd never want to let her go.

'I went into the security sector for a lot of different reasons. When I need a therapist, I'll pay one.'

'You know what I think?' she burst out, stung by his cool derision. 'I think that's precisely why you're a bodyguard. Because you're frightened of getting hurt again. So you've made yourself into this tough, untouchable, macho man whom nobody can get through to, nobody can hurt.'

'Ana, forget the theories,' he advised abruptly, freeing his sleeve from her fingers, swinging away from her. 'The money's good. I enjoy the challenge of the work. These last four

years, maybe I've started freeing myself a little
from total commitment. I've started the
company, stopped being a lone agent. Now I
think it's time we went back. Nina will think I'm
raping you on the beach.'

'Whereas you actually find me so repulsive,
you'd rather swim crocodile-infested waters than
touch me, isn't that it?' she whispered shakily.

He turned back to her.

'Ana, for the love of God...' There was an
aura of contained anger about him that made her
take an involuntary step back. Her heel caught
the hard edge of her discarded sandals, flicking
her sideways in the soft sand, throwing her off
balance. With lightning reaction, Jed dived
forward to catch her. For a frozen, motionless
few seconds, she teetered between recovery and
falling, then she felt her legs give way beneath
her, and somehow they were both sprawled on
the warm sand, and she was cradled in the
strength of his arms.

'Ana...' It was a moan, despairing, softly
furious, torn from him. And she felt as if she
was breaking apart with the force of emotion she
experienced, hearing that moan. Clutching him
convulsively, as if her very life depended on it,
she feverishly responded to the rough seeking of
his hands, the urgent ferocity of his caresses.

He touched her, kissed her as if he'd been
starved for months in a prison and she were his
key to freedom. There was a choked, burning ur-

gency in their embrace, almost a desperation. The sand moulded willingly beneath her, the pink silk of her dress provided little barrier to the sustained assault. Deaf and blind to the other guests, who were quite at liberty to stroll along the moonlit beach, Ana found herself stripped naked, pinned beneath a darkly purposeful Jed whom she suddenly didn't know, and felt slightly afraid of...

'Jed...' Her choked whisper mingled with the warm heat of his breath as she tensed and writhed beneath him.

'You think I find you repulsive?' he ground out, a glitter of bleak humour in his eyes. 'When you're the biggest threat in my life?'

'I—a threat...?' She gasped, heat flooding her as he cupped her breasts with possessive, demanding fingers, squeezed the tight points of her nipples between thumb and finger, raked his fingers down from her breasts to her groin, until the shock waves hurtled through her body like forked lightning. 'Jed, oh, please, oh, God, I can't go on...'

'And I can't stop, not this time, Ana...' he groaned huskily, the heavy fullness of his sex springing free of his clothes as he kicked them to join hers, the remembered sensations thrilling through her from head to toe as he kneed a space for himself between her soft thighs, 'I can't *not* make love to you any longer, Ana...'

'Jed, wait...' It was a weak whisper, torn from the depths of her being, but it was muffled back in her mouth as he covered her lips, kissing her with intense, hungry deliberation.

'Jed...' she gasped as he freed her mouth for a moment, but what she'd been about to say, the important, humiliating confession she needed to make, blurred into nothing as he moved lower. Her fingers tangled convulsively in his hair, gripped jerkily around the strong lines of his head and his shoulders, smoothed down the silken steel of his back, while all the time his mouth moved on her soft nakedness, open and demanding, sucking the aching tips of her breasts, licking and kissing with uninhibited skill all the way down to her navel, across the smooth, vulnerable curve of her stomach, down, down, unthinkably, deliriously, to the intensely feminine privacy of the soft dark curls between her trembling thighs...

'God, Ana...' Having lit the fire, fanned the flames, triggered a hot, liquid meltdown which was roaring through her from her knees to her throat, he lifted his head. He moved swiftly, with the conquering urgency of a pirate, to crush her soft body against the warm sand, a shudder racking him. 'Oh, God, Ana, now, it has to be now...'

'Yes—yes, now...' She sobbed the assent, beyond reason. Wild urgency took over, blinding them both. Heedless of the public beach, uncaring of hidden onlookers, she convulsed in an arch of melting, searing passion as Jed probed, captured, then thrust to the core of her in one mighty, devouring movement which made her cry out in a hoarse, bewildered gasp of pleasure and sharp, piercing pain...

'Oh, no,' he breathed jaggedly, his pupils black and dilated as he lifted his head, gazed down into her huge brown eyes. 'Ana, no—it can't be true, sweetheart...'

'It's true,' she gasped, breathless, her cheeks burning with mortification, but her hormones still soaring high in an invisible sky, her nerve-ends zinging with intense awareness, a volcanic feeling lurking not too far from her emotional surface. 'You're the first. The only one, and *still* the first. Can you believe it? Isn't it just the funniest thing you ever heard...?'

'Oh, Ana.' The deep voice held a cracked, ragged note, half-laughter, half-rebuke. 'This is no joke...'

'No...I know.' She was crying, but she was happy. Winding her arms round his neck, she shuddered with helpless need. 'Jed, keep doing whatever it was you were doing, please?'

'You want me to?' he whispered huskily, cupping her head in his hands, feeling the tears trickle over his fingers and wiping them roughly away. 'You're sure?'

'How can you even *ask* that...?'

'I must be insane...' It was a low groan, but the heat had flared too hot, the shuddering need for completion was too overwhelming. Like hurtling into the Cresta run, there was no going back. The only way was forward, at destructive speed and with terrifying lack of control. Ana closed her eyes and clung to Jed. She felt as if the world was spinning by at the speed of light, the vague but essential destination zooming up ahead with such hectic velocity that she might never survive the impact...

'Jed ... *Jed* ...' She had no idea whose voice it was, muffled, urgent, huskily abandoned, sobbing his name. Then, as the ripples finally stopped convulsing her, physically and emotionally, she had to admit that it had been her own.

Before remorse could strike, before she had time to register the outrageous location of her sexual initiation, Jed recovered his strength sufficiently to scoop her up and wade with her into the Caribbean Sea, dunking them both, half laughing, half protesting, in the silken darkness of the water...

Ana woke in bed, in her airy room in the beach cottage. It was daylight, she registered hazily. Cane blinds diffused the brilliance of the Caribbean sun. The swish of the ocean was rhythmic and soothing. The ceiling fan spun lazily on its axis. She stretched, moved her head, fumbled for her watch. Nearly midday. She'd been so exhausted last night, after the long flight, that she'd fallen asleep the second her head hit the pillow, hadn't she? She subsided on to the pillow again, and struggled with her memory. She was naked. Her body, every inch of her body, felt lazily relaxed, almost boneless. Then memory swirled back, and with it heat, prickling all over. Last night, on the beach... She shivered with a mixture of delight and shame, and then shuddered with remembered pleasure...

And afterwards, that laughing, shivery, sensuous midnight swim. And then, their clothes flung on over wet bodies, the transition here to her room, giving the terrace, and Blake and Nina, a discreetly wide berth. And he'd undressed her again, peeling the damp clothes away, and laid her in bed, climbed in beside her, held her in his arms until she slept...

She sat upright with a jerk. A wary, bubbling happiness was making her light-headed. Sliding long, slender legs to the side, she slipped lightly out of bed, danced into the shower, emerged to inspect rapidly the holiday clothes thoughtfully supplied by Nina from her hotel boutique, as an addition to Ana's hastily assembled belongings. Pulling on a one-piece swimsuit in a silky, copper-coloured material, she added a matching silk T-shirt dress, belted at her small waist with a plaited tan leather belt. Tan leather thong sandals fitted her feet perfectly. At the mirror, she smoothed sunblock on her pale skin, and stroked some gold-brown shadow on her lids. Her face glowed back at her, lit with a subtle inner radiance which made her stare at herself as if she were seeing a stranger in the glass. Her dark brown eyes held a velvety softness. The curve of her mouth looked fuller, more vulnerable...

She was in love, she acknowledged, with a tremor of pure, terrified exultation. This was how it felt. Like...like floating just above the ground. Like shimmering with invisible light...

'Good morning!' Nina's teasing smile held such genuine warmth that Ana had to prevent herself from hugging her. The daytime view from the terrace was as spectacular as the one from her cottage. The blue of the sky arched into sparkling infinity, with the fierce sun at its centre. Beyond a wide, well-watered sward of impossibly green lawn, the roll of the ocean surged with gentle strength to cream softly on to a Persil-white beach, dotted with discreet thatched sunshades, and hedged on all sides by emerald coconut palms and the luxuriant pinks and reds and oranges and yellows of the flowering shrubs and trees...

'This place is paradise,' Ana said simply, her smile so full of joy that Nina blinked. 'Sorry I'm so late waking up! Don't worry about breakfast—just a coffee will do...'

'Nothing of the sort will do,' Nina chided, her hazel eyes moving curiously over Ana's glowing aura, her expression unreadable. 'Come and sit down over here. A royal feast awaits you...!'

'Where's Jed?' Ana barely noticed the array of food, presumably now being served for lunch, and displayed in colourful buffet style. She could hardly contain her impatience to see Jed, but now she felt desperately shy. The euphoria was wearing off. She felt uncertain, butterflies in her stomach. They'd had no time to talk, really talk, about last night, about what it meant to either of them...

'He flew to Miami early this morning.' Nina's statement seemed to hang in the air between them, like an unexploded bomb. Ana could feel her jaw sagging in shock. He'd gone? Flown off somewhere, without telling her? Dismay gave way to anger, and even a shiver of fear.

'He's gone? But... what about me?' She swallowed, struggling to contain her anguish. 'He's supposed to be *protecting* me!' The wail sounded absurdly self-centred. And his protection, or lack of it, wasn't the issue at all. But she could hardly blurt out to Nina her real reason for being upset...

'He's sure you're safe here,' Nina soothed, her gaze sympathetic. 'He and Blake used to work together. He trusts Blake to keep an eye on you until he gets back.'

Ana felt choked with anger and humiliation. She managed a tight smile before she turned away to hide her devastated feelings.

'Thanks a lot. I think I'll skip breakfast, after all. I don't feel very hungry...'

Head high, she retraced her steps back to her cottage, and leaned on the veranda rail, dashing a furious hand over her blurred eyes, dragging a shuddering breath to stop herself from sobbing her heart out.

How could she have let that happen last night? How could she have so little judgement, so little intuition? She was supposed to know how people felt, how the emotions operated. She was a trained actress, for God's sake. So how could she fail so spectacularly, when it came to her own love-life? How could she be so—so dense as to mistake the signs, misread the moment...?

With a shudder of memory, that night at Farthingley loomed back. The night four years ago when Jed had discovered she was a virgin, and calmly advised her to keep the prize for someone who mattered. This time, he'd taken what was so pathetically on offer, but he'd still meant what he said.

Today it was 'business as usual' again, as if nothing had happened. Only this time she didn't even seem to take top priority as his client...

CHAPTER SEVEN

THE sun-lounger on the beach was luxuriously comfortable. The fierce heat of the sun was deflected by the thatched umbrella.

Supine on a scarlet towel, Ana kept her eyes closed, and tried not to think. It was getting easier. One day was beginning to merge into another. It was almost a week since she'd arrived. She might have been abandoned by her bodyguard, but she was being treated with infinite kindness by his friends. And in the absence of anything else to do she was rapidly acquiring a reasonable tan. The simmering indignation at Jed's treatment of her was becoming temporarily blurred by a surfeit of warmth, friendly concern, and enforced laziness . . .

Near her right ear an insect buzzed, but she felt too soporific to stir. The buzz faded to a drone, and then the drone receded. In the distance, waves crashed, the leaves of the tall palm tree close by rattled in the dry breeze. She was nearly asleep, when a male voice said calmly, 'Are you coming snorkelling?'

She sat up so quickly, she almost ricked her neck.

Jed was back. Casually sitting on the sun-lounger next to hers, his features deadpan. She blinked and stared at him, fighting down waves of reaction. He'd gone off without a word, and now he'd turned up again just as abruptly, behaving with nonchalant indifference, as if nothing had happened...

The surge of anger she felt frightened her. She had to keep cool, a small voice of self-preservation warned. If she ranted and accused, he'd probably laugh in her face. She meant nothing to him. What had happened between them had meant nothing to him. She had to remember that, if she was going to survive his company for the remainder of this nightmare...

But she couldn't stop looking at him. His physique in faded green Bermuda swimming-shorts was hard, lean, muscular and golden. All her temporary, newly acquired relaxation had vanished. In the brief scraps of black Lycra that formed her bikini, with her hair plaited loosely down her back, she felt exposed, vulnerable in a raw, painful way, physically and emotionally...

'You've found time to call by and check on your least important *client*, then?' She heard the icy, defensive edge to her voice, and berated herself. What she needed was cool indifference to match his. It was the only way to make him believe she didn't care...

'I wouldn't describe you as "least important",' he returned equably. The lazy gaze moved over her, making her tingle with awareness. The intimacy of their last meeting was still vivid in her mind. Her stomach clenched. The tips of her breasts tightened.

'My father is paying you to be my bodyguard,' she managed, her voice casual, 'and you just fly off and leave me in the charge of a couple of old friends? What have you been doing, anyway?'

Jed's eyes narrowed in bleak amusement.

'Working. On your case. And you were quite safe here, Ana. I wouldn't have left you otherwise.'

'Oh, you're omnipotent, of course. You know all there is to know about everything!'

'Haven't Blake and Nina been looking after you?'

'Of course they have. That's not the point...!' She wanted to hit him. Except that she was afraid the physical contact would prove too much for her composure...

'Blake and I used to work together. I trust him completely.'

'Yes. So Nina told me.' She glared at him frustratedly. Nina had talked a lot about Jed over the past few days. At first Ana had been too proud to show any interest. But then curiosity, a hunger to know more about him, had overruled her pride.

'Nina told me quite a lot of things about you,' she added, keeping her voice level.

'All flattering I hope?' The mockery was cool.

'That depends which way you look at it...' If she'd secretly hoped to goad him into some show of emotion, she was wasting her breath.

'Yeah. I guess it does. So are you coming snorkelling?' Jed's air of uninterest was too authentic to be pretence. Her indignation deepened.

'Don't I even get to know what you've been working on? Whether you've found out who's trying to kidnap me?'

'Not until I've proof beyond any doubt.' Jed stood up easily and gazed down at her. He loomed very large and intimidating above her, and she felt compelled to scramble to her feet to restore some balance to the situation. When she did, she found herself far too close for comfort. Meeting the enigmatic green gaze was the last straw.

'Jed...can we talk?' The words came rushing out, unbidden. So much for cool indifference...

'Talk?' The echo was wry. 'I thought we were already talking.'

'You know what I mean...' Her stomach was churning at his cool amusement. Her face felt hot.

'I do?'

'About that night on the beach...!'

'Oh, *that* night.' His gaze narrowed. 'I thought you'd opt to forget it ever happened.'

'Why would I want to do that?' She was fiercely aware that she was blushing dark red. 'I thought it was the other way round!' She reached down and grabbed her white linen shirt, shrugging it on for protection. She felt altogether too exposed, too vulnerable, standing half naked in front of Jed's hard, unforgiving frame...

'Some things are better left alone,' he agreed.

'Is that why you ran out on me?' she whispered shakily. 'I woke up that morning, feeling...feeling...' The words dried on her lips. How could she admit how she'd felt when she woke up, faced with this calculated display of cruel uninterest? Her pride might be used to taking a battering, where Jed was concerned. Even so, to confess that idiotic, glowing serenity she'd felt that morning would be to abase herself to an unacceptable degree.

'Remorse?' he suggested wryly. His eyes moved over her, narrowed and lazily curious. She felt the familiar shiver of need feathering down her spine. Where his eyes touched, her body tensed. The bikini and shirt were scant protection.

'Not exactly...' She cleared her throat nervously. 'I felt that...that we had something we needed to talk about. You made it clear by jumping on an early plane that you felt differently——'

She made to push past him, but he caught her arm. His grip felt none too gentle.

'What the hell was I supposed to say?' he cut in flatly. A glitter of emotion had darkened his eyes. 'That I broke every rule in my book? That

I let myself be provoked? That I scored nil out of ten for professionalism, self-control, any kind of trained detachment which goes with my job?'

She stared at him, wide-eyed. She didn't know what she'd expected him to say, but it wasn't this. It wasn't this scathing rejection, this denial of any kind of emotional attachment. Words formed on her lips, but she couldn't speak them. The clenched feeling of humiliation and pain was too strong.

'Let go of my arm, Jed...'

'You know what the worst thing is?' he ground out softly, ignoring her plea. 'That you were *still* a virgin! So I don't just breach the rules with one of my own clients, I deflower the maiden into the bargain...!'

Ana couldn't take any more. Stiff and proud, she wrenched free, swerved around the sun-lounger and half ran, half walked away, praying he wouldn't follow, praying she wouldn't break down in tears before she got to her beach cottage, made it to the blessed haven of her room...

Jed reached her side, catching her arm again, propelling her alongside him, steering her along the beach. She was too choked with emotion to speak, she acknowledged miserably. She fought silently to detach herself from his grasp, but he was too strong. And by the time they were inside, with the door shut, she was past tears. White-hot rage had taken over.

'If you think you can push me around, man-handle me...' she spat furiously.

'Ana, I'm sorry...' The curt words were torn from him. Jed's eyes were dark hollows, his jaw tense.

'You're sorry? Well, that's OK, then, isn't it? That makes everything all right again...'

He let her go, and she leaned back on the carved wooden door, gazing at him bleakly. His apology had infuriated her, but at the same time it had knocked some of the anger out of her, as abruptly as it had flared. Now she just felt numb. Something, as far as she could tell in this present numbness, seemed to have died inside her.

'At least that's one thing we have in common,' she added unevenly. 'I'm sorry too.'

'Ana, that night was a mistake.' His voice was measured, as if he was carefully containing his anger. 'If I could undo what happened, I would...'

'You're right, that night was a big mistake,' she agreed, her voice choked. A lump had formed in her throat, and she swallowed hard. 'I—I was annoyed with you for dragging me out here, away from the theatre. I think maybe I—I provoked you as a kind of...silly revenge?'

'Some revenge.'

They gazed at each other in stormy silence.

'You were quite right,' she repeated in a small, wooden voice. 'Right to avoid discussing it. Least said, soonest mended—that's what my mother always said...'

'Mine too.'

Jed spoke with flat lack of expression. Something twisted in her heart as she recalled what Nina had told her during the past few days. But she resolutely smothered the pang. It was hopeless, she conceded. He didn't need her pity, or her sympathy, or her anguish over his long-ago tragedies. And he didn't want her misguided love, either. Jed Steele was a man obsessed. Obsessed with his work. That night had been an aberration. He clearly felt no need, or no desire, to talk about it. He didn't carry the same set of emotional, romantic values as she did. The bitter realisation was like a slap in the face, but it brought her sharply to her senses.

There was a long silence. She fixed her eyes on the cool Italian terracotta tiles on the floor, and willed him to go away.

'Listen—do we *always* have to fight?' Jed's wry humour tore at her emotions. 'Remember how we went sightseeing in Stratford?' he added casually. 'I'd say that was an entire afternoon we managed, without throwing personal insults around...'

With a shrug, she managed a humourless smile. Never let it be said she was slow on the uptake. That night on the beach, whatever its monumental importance for her, was not a subject up for discussion. She'd die rather than show him how much she was hurting inside . . .

'Things have changed since then . . .' she began cautiously.

'Do you still want me to protect you?'

She stared at him in bleak silence.

'Yes . . .'

'Then what else matters?'

'Nothing.' She drew a deep breath. 'Nothing at all. Did you say snorkelling?' She injected a false note of bright enthusiasm into her voice. 'That sounds a wonderful idea . . .'

He reached for her hand, and she stiffened in panic. He linked fingers, stepped back and pulled her gently with him, steering her towards the bathroom.

'Go and take a shower. We'll give snorkelling a miss. We'll check out the culture on the island. Antigua may not boast Shakespeare's birthplace, but it does boast Admiral Horatio Nelson's presence, two hundred years ago. He came out here as Commander of the Leeward Islands Squadron.'

'You don't say?' The sarcasm was weak, but it was the best defence she could manage.

'And if that excitement isn't too much for you, if we take a twenty-minute plane ride across to Nevis we can even visit the Horatio Nelson Museum,' Jed added, a gleam in his eyes, 'and see the house his wife, Fanny Nisbet, brought to her marriage as a dowry.'

'What a walking guidebook you are,' she informed him coolly, turning away and taking refuge in the bathroom. The suggested sightseeing sounded enticing, but she was damned if she'd show Jed her feelings, *any* of her feelings, ever again...

'Couldn't I manage to see the sights without your constant presence?' she called, switching on the shower. 'You don't have to be my bodyguard every second of the day while we're out here. You said so yourself! That's why you felt free to swan off to Miami!'

'I left Blake in charge. Remember? Now that I'm back, you're stuck with me.' Jed sounded coolly amused. 'I'll see you in fifteen minutes.'

She stepped beneath the shower and closed her eyes tightly, bitterly, trying to blot out the mocking smile she imagined on his face...

They took Blake's Jeep. With her hair plaited in a thick blonde rope down her back, feeling cool and refreshed, in a short black linen sundress, Ana tried her very best to enjoy herself. Jed was at his most urbane and charming. He could be brilliantly entertaining company when he put himself out to be. But it was difficult to relax. She knew his company was motivated by professional duty, and not a desire to spend more time with her.

'You never told me how you got to fulfil that big ambition of yours,' Jed said casually as they stopped for a meal after their tour of the island. 'How you got to join the RSC.'

'Pure luck,' she admitted flatly, eyeing their surroundings with a sense of wonder. They'd parked the Jeep in the shade and privacy of a thick clump of palm and seagrape trees, and walked through to a vista so beautiful, it took her breath away. The restaurant was on the edge of a natural lagoon, fringed with exotic vegetation. A graceful white heron skimmed down across the water as she watched, its wings reflecting in the still blue. She was so spellbound, she forgot their conversation.

'You can't just call it luck,' Jed prompted. 'Some talent as well, I imagine?' A waiter was ushering them to a table by the water, handing them large leather-bound menus. There was a pleasant buzz of conversation and laughter, faint strains of steel band music.

'It definitely needs luck to leap straight from one season in rep and a spot of radio work into the RSC.' She met Jed's eyes across the white-clothed table. 'I had a telephone call from my agent one day. Three days and three interviews at the Barbican later, I was invited to join the company. But why are you asking personal questions? Don't pretend you're actually *interested* in my life.'

He gave a wry laugh.

'If they'd been putting on the *Taming of the Shrew*, you'd have landed the lead female role straight away.'

'Thanks. So I believe you've mentioned before.' She smiled sweetly, refusing to rise to the bait. 'And with all this talk of *my* past——'

'What do you want to eat?' Jed interrupted smoothly as the waiter threaded his way towards them through the tables.

'Melon, then swordfish, please,' she said, watching him as he ordered, adding a half-bottle of wine and some mineral water. He'd changed into khaki chinos and a loose black silk shirt. He looked impossibly attractive, withdrawn and untouchable.

When the waiter had gone, Jed eyed her with ominous patience.

'You were saying...?'

It was now or never, she decided, almost losing her nerve.

'I was saying that—that all this interest in *my* past must mean I'm entitled to show an interest in *yours*.'

There was a brief, expressionless silence.

'Go ahead,' he suggested finally. The gleam in his eyes wasn't entirely amused, she decided uneasily. More of a challenge than an invitation.

'Nina told me...' she said rather lamely. The gleam intensified, colder still.

'What did Nina tell you?'

'Your potted life history. That your father was an American academic, your mother an English child psychologist,' she reeled off, parrot-fashion. 'You lived in California until your father died in a car accident, then moved back to London...'

She trailed off as the green gaze drilled into hers.

'Is that it?'

'No,' she confessed, with a short laugh. 'You have a brilliant classics double first from Cambridge. You went into some kind of secret government work before you ended up in your current profession...'

'It sounds as if Nina has been very thorough. Is there any more?'

Ana drew a shaky breath, nodding.

'And when—when you were fifteen you and your mother went to North Cornwall for an autumn holiday, and you nearly died trying to rescue her when a freak wave swept her off some rocks and she drowned...'

There was a brief, taut silence. She swallowed on a sudden lump in her throat. She felt aghast, now that she'd summoned the courage to say it.

'You and Nina have obviously had an enjoyable week,' he commented at last.

Their drinks had arrived. With cool deliberation, Jed filled his glass with mineral water, and poured some of the white wine into her glass. He examined the clear liquid in his glass with a sudden intensity that totally excluded her.

'She only told me about your mother because...' Her heart sank as he turned a cold, unfathomable gaze on her '...because I asked her
to.'

She'd had to beg Nina for the details. But Nina
knew how Ana felt. She'd seen it in her eyes, that
first morning, before Ana had discovered that Jed
had flown off to Miami without telling her. Nina,
Ana knew with a small pang of gratitude, was
on her side...

'You asked her to? Now why did you do that?'
His tone was deadpan.

'Because of...'

'Because of that night on the beach?' he
mocked gently. Colour surged into her face. She
shook her head angrily.

'Not because we made—because we had *sex*,'
she shot back in a low, taut voice. 'I'm not *so*
naïve as to think you owe me your life story for
that!'

'Then what do I owe you, Ana?' She couldn't
fathom his mood at all. It was like having an intimate conversation with a statue.

'It was because of what you said...about
failing your mother. I felt I wanted to try to
understand. Nina told me what happened...'

'And now you understand perfectly.' The icy
derision was devastating. Her throat tightened.
She lifted her glass of wine, and took a
shaky sip.

'No. No, I don't!' she countered unsteadily. 'I don't understand how you could possibly blame yourself. There were witnesses, people who saw the whole thing, saw you on a higher rock when your mother was swept away, saw you dive fully clothed into a rough, dangerous sea! It was a tragic accident, but you couldn't possibly blame yourself because you couldn't save her!'

'Not everything has a rational explanation,' he told her drily, 'and I stopped blaming myself for my mother's death quite a few years ago. So let's just eat our meal and find something else to talk about, shall we?'

They ate in strained silence for a while. The melon was deliciously juicy. The swordfish was chunky and tender, with a spicy Creole-style sauce. Ana sipped her wine, and tried unsuccessfully to convince herself that the silence was amicable. She'd wanted so much to be able to comfort him about the tragedy over his mother. But he was so locked up inside. She couldn't get close. She'd never get close enough.

'I thought you suggested a truce without fighting?' she managed at last. Her brown eyes were expressionless as she tilted her chin up to face him.

He gave a short, humourless laugh.

'Yes, I did, didn't I? But if ever there were two people destined to fight, they're you and me.'

'Only because you're paranoid about revealing even a fraction of your real self!'

Jed didn't bother to answer. The green gaze was lidded as he stared at her across the table. She felt his gaze move lazily on her, and every inch of her body seemed to react to it. Goosebumps broke out on her arms and thighs, even in the heat of the Caribbean evening. She felt a stab of angry resentment. His impassive non-communication was more than just infuriating. It was insulting. And it was hurtful...

'Besides,' she countered, making her voice harder to mask her feelings, 'fighting's one way of passing the time, isn't it? A way of livening up this restricted feeling of being a prisoner in paradise?'

Jed's face hardened a fraction, but his eyes remained steady.

'You're feeling restricted?' He sounded drily sardonic. 'At least you're not gagged and blindfolded in some damp cellar, wondering whether you'll ever see the sun again.'

She stared at him in shocked silence. The lazy, hedonistic warmth of the Caribbean seemed to mock her in the speechless moment stretching between them.

He summoned the waiter for the bill, and stood up abruptly.

'Let's go.' The terse note in his voice was disturbing. Uneasily, she followed him out of the brightness of the restaurant, towards the shady copse of trees. She realised that while they'd been talking, eating and drinking the rapid Caribbean night had fallen. She'd meant to watch the stunning sunset over the lagoon, as Jed had suggested. She'd missed it, intent instead on fighting off that cool, derisive gaze which seemed to empty her mind and tie her tongue into knots...

'I'm sorry. I don't know why I said that,' she said tightly. There was a hard lump in her throat.

'I do.'

She stared at him again, through the gathering darkness, resentment warring with shame.

'Do you?'

'Provocation. That's how you while away your idle moments, isn't it? You needle a reaction out of someone else. Don't try it again, Ana,' he warned softly, silken steel in his voice, 'because it won't work this time.'

'You're wrong.' She shook her head quickly, anger surging through her. 'You think you know so much about me, but you're *wrong*!'

'Am I? I know what a good actress you are,' he reminded her ruthlessly. 'I watched you in all your three plays at Stratford.'

'So you think I'm *always* acting?' she challenged unsteadily. 'You think everything I do is a—a performance? You think I'm so shallow? Maybe...maybe you think I was play-acting when we made love? That I pretended to feel pleasure...?'

Her face was burning as he turned to look at her, but the husky goad seemed to electrify him.

They'd reached the Jeep, and he stopped, swinging round and taking hold of her. The touch of his fingers on her bare arm was sweet torture. Trickles of furious desire threaded along her nerve-ends.

'You never stop, do you?' he rasped, jerking her so that she was imprisoned between him and the bonnet of the Jeep. He was angry, she registered dimly, very angry. Why? Because she'd dared to relate Nina's sympathetic story of his traumatic past? Or because he'd despised her for that ill-advised comment on being trapped in paradise? Or was it because of what she'd just said?

'Stop what?' she breathed unsteadily. 'Trying to communicate?'

'Trying to score points, get your own way, seek attention...'

'That's not fair, Jed...!' She writhed in his grip, without success. He kissed her hard on the mouth, deepening his assault until it became a sensual invasion, firing darts of pleasure all over her. Then heat swept through her, from her toes to her forehead, as he caught her at the waist and lifted her, bodily, on to the warm metal of the Jeep's bonnet, then stepped closer to lodge his hard body against her.

She froze, not daring to move. The short black dress, with its full swirly skirt, had flared out and ridden high. Her bare thighs were trapped on either side of Jed's lean hips.

'Jed, let me down...' she whispered, aghast
'Stop this...'

'Why?' he goaded softly, raking hard hand
down her slender back and spanning her hips with
his fingers. 'Isn't this what you want? A little
excitement to liven up this restricted life you're
leading?'

To her intense horror, he bent his head to tra
small, tantalising, intense kisses from her clavicl
to the swell of her breasts at the scoop neck o
her dress. Running his hands around her waist
he pulled her closer, sliding his fingers up t
caress the jut of her nipples beneath the blac
fabric. The sensations were so conflicting, s
outrageously arousing, she gasped out loud. In
voluntarily, she stopped struggling, let her finger
lace into the thickness of his hair, then spla
along the taut width of his shoulders beneath th
silk shirt, and with a mixed jolt of fear and ex
ultation she heard him give a muffled groan o
desire. The black linen dress felt as flimsy as
silk petticoat. Through the covering, his lip
sought and found one hardening nipple and bi
gently. Shuddering helplessly, she felt hersel
melt, catch fire, flare into a thousand sparks o
need.

Heedless of her surroundings, somethin
deeply primitive had taken her by surprise. Sh
was sinking under it, yielding to Jed's bold as
sault, on a sensual tide, out of control...

She was shivering uncontrollably as he pushed her back across the bonnet of the Jeep. He smoothed the short skirt up to her waist, raking possessive hands from her splayed knees to her groin, and tracing their path with his lips.

'Jed...' It was a choked cry of reproof and a gasp of sheer, torturing wanting.

'God knows what you do to me,' he growled raggedly. His thumbs had hooked inside the brief white lace triangle of her panties, their intimate exploration arrogantly sure, triggering a hot eruption of desire, right at the tender core of her being.

'Jed...please, this is...oh, God, Jed...' She wriggled helplessly, dizzy with sensation.

He lifted her forward again, searching her face before he crushed her into his arms. Ana could hardly breathe. Her pulses were racing, her heart pounding so hard that she could hear it blend with his. In the semi-darkness, his hard face had looked like a stranger's. The heat of desire in his eyes had scorched her.

'I want you, Ana,' he grated against her hair. 'To hell with rules and ethics. I need you, tonight...'

'Oh, no...I...' Could she withstand another lovemaking session? Knowing there was no love involved? Could she take any more emotional battering? Panic was hammering through her now. She was almost incoherent as he dragged her down from the bonnet and thrust her into the Jeep. He gunned the engine into life, and they drove back to the hotel in tense silence, rumbling over the bumpy roads, swerving around dark bends. They pulled up outside the hotel, swept to a halt at the entrance.

He turned to look at her as they stopped. She had no idea how she must look, mussed and dishevelled and bemused by the volcanic passion outside the restaurant. But Jed looked devastating. Catching the wry light in his eyes, seeing that flash of a smile against the dark of his face, she felt as if, in that split-second, some true communication had taken place between them. Whether it was just desire, or something deeper, suddenly the bond between them was so strong it was almost tangible. Her heart expanded and altered, from miserable grey into brilliant colour.

'Jed...' she began huskily, then stopped. Blake must have been waiting for them, because he emerged from the hotel entrance and ran down the steps, darted between the lush royal palms and beneath the arch of purple bougainvillaea, and wrenched open Jed's door. There was such a grim expression on his face that Ana's words died on her lips.

'Some bad news, I'm sorry, Ana,' he began in a low voice. 'Your father——'

'He hasn't been kidnapped?' she burst out, hysteria rising at the explanation leaping to her brain. She saw Jed's hands tighten convulsively on the wheel. The knuckles had gone white. He cares, she registered distantly, amid the panic. He does have feelings . . .

'No. Not that.' Blake's blue eyes were kind, his weatherbeaten face was furrowed with concern. 'But he's in hospital. I'm afraid he's had a coronary, a heart attack . . .'

CHAPTER EIGHT

'DAD?' Are you awake? Can you hear me?' Bending over her father's bed in the private hospital room, Ana caught hold of the strong, gnarled hands and clasped them tightly. Her voice was so thick with suppressed tears, she wondered if he'd recognise her, so she added rather unnecessarily, 'It's me, Ana!'

'Yes, my love. I do know my own daughter's voice.'

To Ana's astonished delight, her father even managed a flash of his normal sense of humour as he slowly opened his eyes. 'And just hearing it makes me feel better!'

'You gave me such a fright,' she chided huskily, stroking his hands, smiling through her tears. 'The nurses said you were much better but, seeing you lying here with all these...these monitors and things, I thought...' She gulped, and took a mental grip on herself, finishing up more sharply, 'Just don't you dare do that again!'

'Do what—fall asleep? I'm supposed to be recuperating, darling. Sleep's good for me. You've gone nicely brown.' Looking rather pale and haggard against the pillows, William French moved his eyes wryly over his daughter's appearance, taking in the flat laced boots, dark green leggings and floppy black V-neck sweat-shirt with a glint of humour. 'Always the little bohemian, but at least you're glowing. Jed's looking after you well. I can see that...'

'He's stalking my every move, you mean,' she said, unable to keep a tighter note from her voice, 'setting my nerves on edge so I can't sleep at night...'

'He'll catch whoever it is soon.' Her father spoke with quiet confidence. 'I know he's had his company working on forensic stuff...' He struggled for breath slightly, and Ana clutched his hand anxiously. 'Clues taken from those notes. He'll solve the problem. Then you'll be free... to get some sleep again.'

The double meaning, and the knowing gleam in her father's eyes, made her blush involuntarily.

'Dad...!'

'Don't play-act with me, my girl,' he said softly, laughing, then wheezing alarmingly, bringing a frowning nurse scuttling in. 'Don't pretend there's nothing between you and Jed Steele, because I wasn't born yesterday, and you could cut the air with a knife when you're together...'

'Mutual dislike can cause quite an atmosphere,' she agreed, dropping a farewell kiss on his forehead to hide the bleak unhappiness in her eyes, and avoiding the nurse's curious gaze. 'I'll call in again in the morning. And get well fast...'

'You can rely on it, darling.'

Jed was waiting outside the door, lounging against the wall, one of his deadpan watchful expressions masking any emotion. In denims, black polo-neck and suede bomber jacket, he was disturbingly good to look at. Far from fading, her awareness of him just kept deepening. But she kept her eyes studiedly detached as she met his enquiring gaze.

'He's going to be all right, I think,' she said cautiously, a crease of worry between her eyes, 'but that was the worst twenty-four hours of my life!'

'He's a strong man, very fit for his age,' Jed agreed calmly as they found the car and drove back along high-banked Dorset lanes to Farthingley, 'but stress can do a lot of harm. He's been worried about this kidnap threat...'

She glanced at Jed as they pulled up in front of Farthingley's half-timbered frontage. She hadn't been entirely truthful with her father, she acknowledged guiltily, implying that Jed was getting seriously on her nerves, pretending that she couldn't wait to be free of her 'bodyguard'...

If she'd been honest, she'd have confessed that being in his company was beginning to feel as natural as breathing, even if he did keep an insulting distance between them, even if he did mask his feelings behind his professional expertise, even if he did make critical, disparaging remarks about her character, and even if he did despise her for that night on the beach in Antigua...

He'd been supportive and protective since she'd heard the news about her father. Maybe that was why she was beginning to rely on his presence. While she'd dithered with panic and distress, he'd made quick-fire arrangements, booked them on the next flight home via Miami, rung the hospital, reassured her that her father was improving...

If she'd been infatuated with him four years ago, now she had to admit the bitter truth. She was hopelessly in love with him. Masochistic, scarcely believable, but true...

The rare, brief moments when they'd relaxed together, when they'd talked, like equals, like friends, had proved to her that they had things in common. Proved that Nina, with her glowing stories about him, was right. Underneath his tough exterior, Jed was a great guy. But presumably only towards people he respected. And it was obvious, Ana reflected painfully, that the more he got to know about her, the less he liked. The fact that she could feel such a depth of love for someone who felt only disdain and contempt for her was unnerving...

Sexual desire was the answer, she told herself with a stab of shame. The sexual attraction she felt towards Jed was so powerful it terrified her. But even so she found it hard to believe that she'd done what she'd done with him, on the beach...and succumbed so easily to his powerful assault that night at the lagoon...

The shock of hearing about William had swiftly extinguished that searing desire. And since then Jed had reverted to his neutral, contained detachment. If he thought about it at all, he gave no sign. No doubt he blamed her for provoking him again. And the gulf between them had drifted so wide, she could hardly believe that their wild intimacy had actually happened...had it been a vivid, feverish dream? Had she become such a frustrated, thwarted little novice that she'd conjured up the whole episode in her head?

'I'm grateful for all your help,' she said abruptly, looking at Jed with a slightly hectic glitter in her eyes. 'If I haven't said that before, I'm sorry. But I am. Very grateful...'

'Stop thanking me, and stop apologising,' he suggested, his gaze unfathomable. 'It's part of the job. I'm being paid for all this, remember?'

'Oh, Jed,' she breathed, angry frustration tearing through her. 'Can't you ever stop hiding behind your blasted job?'

'Do you want a kidnap threat hanging over your head indefinitely?'

'Of course not, but...'

'I think I know who's doing it.'

They'd reached the front door, and she stopped dead in the entrance to Farthingley. His cool statement made her gape at him in astonishment.

'You do? When did you find out?'

'I did some checking when I was in Miami. Someone who should have been safely locked away is no longer locked away.'

'Who?' She was ashamed to find that her mouth had dried. Her head was thumping nervously.

'An ex-colleague of your father's. A scientist.'

To cover her vague feelings of panic, she glared at him in baffled fury. 'Why should he want to harm me?'

'For similar reasons to why he wanted to harm your father four years ago, I imagine.'

'Which were?'

'The man is demented,' Jed said briefly. 'He thought William had stolen one of his ideas.'

'Then why don't you just—just arrest whoever it is and leave me in peace?'

'Because I need hard evidence. Jumping to conclusions is the easiest road to bankruptcy or imprisonment in my profession.'

'Oh, great!' she exploded, marching towards the stairs, fairness or logic deserting her. 'So I have you trailing around after me until you're satisfied that your own back is covered, and your end-of-year accounts won't suffer a set-back?'

He'd followed her up to her room, and she turned to find him casually leaning on the door-jamb. Unthinkingly, her mind full of confused possibilities, she crossed to sit on the bed, and began kicking off her boots, and peeling her sweatshirt over her head, ready for a quick shower before dinner. Suddenly she froze, then yanked the sweatshirt down, appalled at herself. A wave of heat prickled her neck at his wry expression.

'Should I hide behind my job now, or am I being invited as audience to an impromptu strip-tease?' he enquired, his mouth twisting. But his humour looked dangerous. There was a darker gleam in his eyes. She felt herself tense, a rigid, stomach-clenching tension which almost stopped her from breathing.

'No, you are not!' she managed, her face flaming. 'I was miles away then...distracted...'

'Don't apologise,' he murmured huskily, levering himself away from the door, pushing it shut, and walking towards her. 'And don't stop on my account...'

The shivers were like tiny stabs of pain, all over her body. Jed's gaze was smokily amused as he gazed down at her.

'You want me to *strip* in front of you?' she whispered, with choked fierceness. 'What is your problem, Jed? One day you're interested, the next day you don't want to know me.'

'My problem,' he said softly, his voice thickening, 'is that you're the road to hell, Ana. My good intentions are paving it every minute I spend in your company. I want you so damned badly, I'm getting no sleep at night...'

'Bodyguards aren't supposed to sleep,' she croaked, her heart hammering so frantically that she could hear it vibrating against her ribs. 'Are they?'

'Everyone needs sleep...' The look in Jed's eyes was melting her stomach, melting her thighs. They were talking, but the words they were saying were meaningless. The real communication was taking place in taut, tense silence. The challenge held so many layers of meaning, so many strands of emotion, she felt her control flip. With trembling fingers, unsure if she felt furious, faint, or just wildly defiant, she peeled up the sweatshirt with one graceful, sweeping movement, and tossed it on to the bed. Her breasts heaving with suppressed emotion, she stood in front of him, chin high, brown eyes blazing her own challenge, blonde hair tumbling around her shoulders, her nipples small, clenched buds pushing shamelessly against the ivory satin of her bra.

Jed's eyes had darkened. The brilliance of the green was almost eclipsed by a hungry, deepening blackness which shook her to the depths of her soul. With a muttered oath, crudely explicit, he reached to unhook the front fastening of the bra and peel the fabric from the high jut of her breasts.

She made a sound, a moan in her throat, as he reached for her, took the swell of her breasts in his hands, pulled on the swollen, crimson tips, caressing the creamy flesh with a shudder of emotion, raw and unmistakably urgent.

'Ana...' He slipped his hands beneath her armpits, catching her to him, his thumbs torturing her into shivering need as he circled them against the weight of her breasts. Dropping his head, he took one heated nipple in his mouth, bit gently, sucked with growing demand. She was buckling, dizzy with angry desire, hardly believing it, unable to control it...

'Jed, for pity's sake,' she croaked unsteadily, her head falling back, the carnal eroticism of Jed's assault emptying her brain, numbing her defences...

'I want you... If you think I've forgotten that night on the beach, it's branded in my mind, it won't go away... God, Ana, I want you so much I'm on fire...' The deep voice was soft and rough and devastatingly urgent. The green leggings, stretchy, offering no resistance to his seeking fingers, were arrogantly tugged down, her brief satin panties disappearing along with them. Shuddering from head to toe now, as if she had a fever, Ana shut her eyes in acute despair as he pushed a rough, denim-clad knee between her thighs, cupped the softness of her buttocks with possessive need, exploring the hidden heat with intimate thoroughness until she felt herself burning up, white-hot and surrendering...

As if from a huge distance, Ana heard the shrill bell of the telephone ringing in another part of the house, then silence, then Ellen's voice calling up the stairs. The distance voice crashed indecently into the heady, ragged breathing in the bedroom. Slowly, like someone drowning, Ana collected her wits, hauled herself back from the brink, pushed herself away from him. She sank weakly on to the bed and tried, rather belatedly and idiotically, to cover herself with her hands.

Jed's curse was terse and unrepeatable.

'You'd better go and have that shower,' he suggested, harshly bleak. 'I'll go and tell Ellen you'll ring them back...'

'Yes, yes...oh, just get out!' she whispered, shaking, clutching her arms round herself. 'Just get out and leave me alone...!'

'I'm on my way. But are you angry with me?' he queried grimly. 'Or with yourself?'

'With...*everything*!' she flung at him chokingly. But she watched him leave with her eyes blinded by tears of self-disgust...

'It was one of the stage managers from the theatre,' she informed Jed later, in answer to his cool question. She'd showered, dressed, composed herself and returned the call, before joining him for dinner in the oak-panelled dining-room. With just the two of them eating there, the room seemed vast, and yet the pool of light at their end of the table seemed unbearably intimate. Ana couldn't help thinking of that night four years earlier, when she'd flounced in here, in her short skirt and extra perfume, eager to impress the devastating stranger she'd met earlier in the herb garden...

'Are you going to tell me what he wanted?' Jed persevered wryly as she picked up her spoon and tried her soup.

'Lana Stewart has cracked three ribs in a car accident. They want me to take over my understudy role...'

Jed's eyes narrowed across the dinner-table. Ellen had gone to some lengths to produce a delicious meal. She'd proudly announced that they were to enjoy home-made tomato and basil soup, followed by succulent roast lamb with mint sauce and new potatoes, and the promise of one of her apple pies with clotted cream to follow. But the tension buzzing in the air was drying Ana's throat, making the soup taste like water...

'When?'

'Tomorrow. I have to go back to the theatre tomorrow...' She said it with a degree of uncertainty. But not because of the kidnap threats—because of her father. 'I—I'll check with the hospital first. See Dad. But it's an opportunity I've hardly dared think about. As—as long as Dad's continuing to improve, I have to do it...'

'I agree.' His cool agreement made her jaw drop in surprise.

'You do?'

'Sure. Why not?' His mouth twisted slightly. 'It's a golden opportunity.'

She lowered her spoon. His cool sarcasm had been half expected, but it still hurt. She stared at him, in the muted light from the low pendent lamp above them. He'd swapped the denims for black chinos, but still wore the black polo-neck. He looked hard, brooding, judgemental, derisive, everything she'd come to expect of him...and yet...

'You don't need to come with me,' she said quickly, snatching up her wine glass with slightly unsteady fingers. 'If you're pretty convinced you know who's been sending those silly notes, then that's that, isn't it?'

'Not entirely, no.'

'Jed, I need to get away!' she burst out, sipping some wine then clicking the glass back on to the polished refectory table with a shaky click. I need to get away from *you* she added silently, seething. From what you're doing to me...

'I'm feeling...stifled, smothered...' she finished up tensely. 'I can't stand this any longer...'

'It won't be for much longer, Ana,' he countered coldly. The green gaze was bleak. 'But the danger still exists.'

'Right,' she snapped, goaded into defiance. 'So I have to endure the ridicule of the rest of the cast all over again? Just so you can earn your full fee and keep in with my father?'

There was an ominous flicker in Jed's eyes as he held her stormy gaze across the table. He let his eyes slide down over her slender neck and the creamy-gold swell of her breasts, above the deep scoop neck of her short emerald silk sheath dress. She'd dressed up for dinner tonight, spurred on by a need to boost her battered confidence. She'd taken extra care with her hair, wound into a neat French plait, and with her make-up, a subtle blend of hazel eyeshadow and a light fluff of coral-gold blusher. She'd clipped on heavy gold hoop earrings, threaded a lustrous golden pendant round her neck. She'd unconsciously dressed to seduce, so that she could manage the dubious victory of fending off any further advances...

But now she moistened her lips nervously. He made her nervous, watching her with that contained, implacable gaze. She was so on edge, so brittle with tension, she felt as if she might crack apart...

Why was she in such a state? She knew why, she admitted bitterly. Quite apart from the shameful weakness she'd shown in her bedroom earlier, her pathetically feeble show of sexual desire, there was the humiliating knowledge that, while she harboured this secret, senseless infatuation, Jed's sudden flares of desire were merely knee-jerk reactions to her thoughtless provocation. Sexual desire for men was different. The emotions didn't have to be involved. But her own stupidity was mind-boggling. If Ellen hadn't called upstairs, she'd have let him make love to her again, and nearly died with the bittersweet excitement of it again—she'd have let it happen all over again, and *wanted* it to happen fiercely and triumphantly, even when she had ample evidence that he cared nothing about her, didn't even *like* her very much...

She was crazy. He was driving her insane...

'I'm disappointed, Ana,' he told her with barbed softness. 'I thought you might have grown up. Found a way round your only-child ego. But the only person you're interested in is still Miss Anastasia French, superstar in the making.'

Her stomach in knots, she gave a stiff shrug. She'd sounded spoiled-brattish. She knew she had. But she hardly knew what she was saying any longer...

'The way you see me is *your* opinion,' she told him, her voice level as she controlled her temper with an effort. 'You see what you want to see. Based on *your* twisted beliefs. But that's *your* problem, not mine. Do you mind if we just concentrate on eating Ellen's meal?' She managed a passable impression of a sweet, uninterested smile. 'If I don't finish it all up, she'll be hurt, and I love Ellen dearly...'

'Fine by me.'

'Oh, and incidentally, do you mind if I lock my bedroom door? I don't want any unwanted intruders.'

'Don't worry,' he retorted ruthlessly, a glint of mocking amusement defeating her poise, 'I'll make sure I earn my fee. I'll stand guard outside your door all night, Ana...'

* * *

The roar of applause was like a massive waterfall, filling the auditorium with a rushing, swelling crescendo. A fourth curtain call, Ana thought gratefully, adrenalin coursing through her as she clasped the hands of her fellow actors and sank into another deep bow. She hadn't been a complete flop, then, as a stand-in for the main female role...

Tonight, she'd flung herself into the coveted role, and she didn't need the crowd's reaction to tell her that the play had been well-received, that her final ringing speech had been well-received. Whatever the trigger for this ecstatic response, it was magical, Ana thought, flinging herself into another bow, and then lifting her face to smile incandescently at the sea of white faces and moving hands, her long thick hair cascading back down her shoulders, bare in the daringly low-cut amber taffeta of her costume. Poor Lana, she reflected with a stab of guilt, laid up with painfully cracked ribs, missing out on this tremendous elation tonight—but lucky Lana, to have this role to play for real...

Where was Jed? She'd wondered if she might see him, towards the front of the stalls. When he'd told her he was watching tonight's performance, she'd had mixed feelings. Half apprehension, half foolish, stubborn pleasure...

She rushed through changing, modestly fenced the flurry of congratulations and the words of praise from cast and crew, conscious only of a need to see Jed. Why Jed, for heaven's sake? she chided herself furiously as she made it down to the stage door, clad in velvet hat and velvet jacket, and prepared to leave.

He wasn't inside the stage door. And he wasn't waiting outside, either, as a rapid scan of the autograph hunters told her. Annoyed at herself for her stubborn longing to share her triumph with him, she left a message with the night receptionist. She was at the pub if he wanted her. With that, she marched out into the cool October night.

There'd been a torrential rainstorm last night. The River Avon was flowing high, almost bursting its banks in some places, she noticed, gazing at its inky blackness beneath the willows as she walked quickly towards the pub, just a couple of hundred yards from the theatre. A chilly wind had blown up, and she hugged her coat round her, and tucked her black scarf more tightly round her neck. What had happened to Indian summers? she wondered briefly. They seemed to have plunged straight from summer into winter this year...

Ana was aware of feeling perfectly safe, walking the short distance to the pub. The streetlights weren't exactly illuminating, but she was hardly alone. There were several groups of people walking along the pavement, going the same way as she was. Mostly they'd be the audience who'd been watching the play at the Swan theatre, which finished earlier than the programme in the main theatre.

She became aware of the sinister aura of the man behind her only as she felt an arm go around her shoulders. With a stab of surprise, she turned, her heart jerking, expecting, for some foolish reason, to see Jed. Instead she found herself looking into the eyes of a rather overweight man, thirtyish, with pale skin and fair, greasy hair, and large, staring blue eyes.

'Hi Ana,' he murmured. She was just wondering where she could have seen him before, whether she knew him, when he clapped an oily hand over her mouth as she opened it to speak. 'Did you think you were *safe*?'

Her muffled shriek alerted none of her fellow pub-bound walkers. Propelled by an unpleasant display of male strength, she found herself being frogmarched across the road, between the parked cars, and through a gap in the wall to the gardens bordering the river. The full, flowing blackness of the water loomed ahead.

Panic, fury and sheer terror crowded and jostled in her brain. Fighting every inch of the way, she felt something hard prod the small of her back, and her nerve-ends tingled with fresh fear.

'I've got a knife,' her attacker purred, 'so stop kicking and scratching, bitch...'

The hand was briefly taken from her mouth, and with every last scrap of energy she possessed she yelled, '*Jed*...!' before ducking, twisting, somehow managing to free herself. Her hat blew off as she ran, blindly, fuelled by the need to survive. The darkness of the night seemed to close in around her, menacing, awaking her latent terror of the darkness itself, as well as her terror of the man lumbering furiously after her.

'*Jed*...!' She shrieked his name into the wind, into the night air, as the man lunged, grabbed her arm, and she tore free again, raced ahead, looking fearfully over her shoulder, not seeing where she was running, until abruptly the ground became water...

With a scream of fright, she felt herself falling, clutched wildly at the air, connected briefly with some ineffectual willow branches until they snapped and failed her, and then she was flying headlong into the icy, foul-tasting darkness of the river...

CHAPTER NINE

ANA surfaced, spat out water, tried to scream, submerged again. The river was fast-flowing, with a surprisingly strong current. Swimming against it was hampered by water-logged boots, the cumbersome velvet jacket. The cold was intense. It felt like being packed in ice, and bound by invisible clingfilm...

Only seconds after she'd hit the water she heard a splash as her pursuer leaped in after her. Flailing wildly, she kicked with her legs, felt something, maybe river-weed, trap her ankle, and panicked, going under the dank water again. Did your life flash by when you were on the point of drowning? Ana wondered disjointedly, bursting to the surface again and snatching air into her lungs with huge, painful gasps. She couldn't possibly die now, when she still had so much of it to live...

When a strong pair of arms caught her from behind, lifted her against what felt like a hard male body, she shrieked, struggling frantically.

'No! Let go of me, you bastard——*help*!'

'Ana, you dim-wit. Stop struggling; it's me...'

Jed's voice. Harsh, laboured for breath, but still very much in control. Jed's arms round her, guiding her towards the bank, where a number of passers-by from the theatre seemed to have gathered to watch a real-life drama enacted before their horrified eyes.

'Oh thank God,' she gasped, clinging to him tightly, feeling his strength. 'I thought you were that fat, spotty man—he knew my name, he tried to grab me...'

'Save your breath until we get out of this blasted river,' Jed advised raggedly, propelling her towards a cluster of low-hanging branches, and catching hold of the lowest one. The water swirled past them, the current catching at her clothes, plucking hungrily at her. With great initiative, someone broke away from the growing group of people on the riverbank and ran for a boat hook, and slowly, through mud and slime, they were hauled from the river, and Ana found herself in a sodden, gasping heap on the dark grass, coughing and spluttering, while someone wrapped a coat round her...

She looked up, dazed and confused. A police car had drawn up, its blue light flashing importantly. There suddenly seemed to be people everywhere, but Jed appeared to have abandoned her. Then she saw him, still in his Levis, but shirtless and barefoot, and apparently immune to the cold, squatting beside the inert form of a man lying spread-eagled on the grass. At the same time he was talking and gesticulating with familiar economy of style to the two policemen who'd arrived to gaze down in polite suspicion at the motionless body at their feet. She couldn't hear the conversation, but then Jed straightened up, turned his back on the police and came to help her to her feet.

'Who's the body?' she asked through chattering teeth.

'The jerk who tried to grab you. And he's not a body. He's just unconscious for a short time, that's all.'

'What happened to him?'

'He and I had a disagreement.' Jed's expression was harshly humorous, but she found herself fleetingly picturing the brief contest and feeling relieved not to have witnessed it. Even though she had no sympathy with her would-be attacker, the thought of being on the wrong end of Jed Steele's lethal strength sent tremors down her spine...

'He's the one I was telling you about,' Jed went on tersely. 'He's an American. His name is Desmond Carter...'

'The demented scientist?'

'Yes. Ana, we'll talk about this later...' Jed had found his own suede jacket, and wrapped that around her too, ignoring her shivering protests that he needed it more, his eyes dark with concern.

'Are you OK?' he added, more gently.

'Fine. Swimming fully dressed in flooded rivers is my favourite way of unwinding.' She laughed shakily. But she clung to him, trembling violently, and with a low, stifled curse under his breath Jed jerked her into his arms and crushed her there tightly, holding her hard against the muscular length of his body with a silent urgency that made her heart beat faster, regardless of her drenched and frozen condition.

'Don't *ever* put me through that again,' he whispered in her ear, the mixture of anger and emotion in his voice a heady combination.

'You didn't have to dive in and rescue me,' she managed huskily, lifting her head and tilting it back to look into his face, 'but thanks anyway...'

'Ana...'

'And if you dare say it's all part of the job,' she added hoarsely, 'I'll jump back in...'

'Damn it to hell,' he ground out, tightening his grip so that she could hardly breathe, 'I thought you were going to drown...'

'And then you wouldn't have got paid?' she taunted, shivering. 'You'd have done all this work for nothing?'

His answer was unrepeatable. Abruptly, he bent his head and kissed her forcefully, almost brutally, and with her fingers clinging to the cool, taut muscle of his shoulders the response she felt was so intense, so equal in every way to Jed's violent emotion, that the world, with its small cluster of curious and fascinated onlookers, its patiently waiting police coughing meaningfully behind them, its unconscious would-be kid-napper sprawled on the grass, was completely blotted out...

* * *

'Why did you leave the stage door without me?' Jed was just as relentless as the police had been, in his pursuit of the full facts, she reflected, hours later. A suggested trip to hospital had been curtailed by Jed's cool insistence that they were both fit enough to go straight back for hot baths and a change of clothes at the hotel, and give statements to the police afterwards. The suite they'd been given was a different one, but equally luxurious. It was nearly three o'clock in the morning, but the log fire was burning cheerfully. They'd rung the private hospital near Farthingley, checked that her father was all right. Tomorrow, they'd go and give him the news in person. Let him know the kidnap threat was over. That its perpetrator was caught...

She shivered involuntarily. She was carefully sipping a glass of brandy Jed had given her, and the fiery liquid was burning its own heat inside her, but she still shivered every time she thought of the horror of the attack, the sheer terror of falling in the river...

'Why did you do it, Ana?'

'Because you weren't there?' she suggested cautiously. Why *had* she marched off on her own? Because of the high she'd been experiencing, after taking over the lead role? Because of a defiant need to demonstrate her independence, show she wasn't afraid any more?

'I told you to wait.'

'I did. You still weren't there.'

'I got trapped in the crush coming out of the theatre,' Jed informed her stonily, his green gaze gleaming with suppressed amusement at her stubborn defiance. 'I opted against mowing down a group of elderly ladies with walking sticks and trampling over a bunch of Japanese tourists...'

'You could have come round the backstage way...'

'And risk incurring the displeasure of Miss Anastasia French, star of the show?' he queried tersely.

She lowered her eyes, reluctant to concede that she'd begged him not to barge his way around backstage and provoke even more teasing and ribbing from cast and crew...

'There'd have been no problem if you'd done as you were told,' he added flatly. Leaning back in the chair on the opposite side of the fire, he flexed his shoulders with a weary ripple of muscle. He was wearing the black chinos and charcoal silk shirt that he'd dressed in for their interview with the police. She'd pulled on her warmest clothes after a steaming hot bath, and was now sweating slightly in denims, raspberry-coloured brushed-cotton shirt and a floppy, thickly ribbed jumper the same colour. She'd plaited her damp hair after washing the dank river water out of it, and catching sight of herself in the dressing-table mirror, she'd thought with dismay that she looked about sixteen...

'Will you stop lecturing me like a pompous schoolmaster?' she demanded softly. 'I'm sorry

I left the theatre alone. I was wrong. Stupid. Spoiled. Everything you say. You saved my life, and I'm prepared to grovel at your feet in any case. You were the hero of the hour. My knight on a white charger, just the way I used to fantasise about you...'

Her voice cracked on a note of bitter humour, and she stopped. Jed had put down his own brandy, and leaned forward, forearms on his knees.

'At least now you've got to know me better you can forget the fantasies,' he said shortly.

'Oh, yes,' she agreed, forcing a lightness to her voice. 'I certainly can. So tell me, all that stuff you told the police about this crazy Desmond— was it true?'

'Do you think I would lie to the police?' Jed's mouth twisted slightly.

'I suppose not. It's just that it's so hard to believe. That someone I don't know, never met, could want to threaten me like that...' How could she say that the information had rocked her, shaken her in some idiotic way, without sounding like the hopelessly spoiled, over-protected child that Jed had always labelled her?

'It was William he wanted to damage. Four years ago, he was sending death threats. I tracked him down, and had him tucked away in a secure sanatorium in America. This time, he didn't just blame William for stealing his "scientific secrets". He blamed him for having him locked up in the sanatorium. He wanted revenge on your

ather, by threatening to harm you.' The deep
oice was slightly gentler.

'But my father had never stolen any of this
cientist's precious ideas in the first place!'

'No. He hadn't. Desmond Carter is what's
nown as a paranoid schizophrenic, suffering
rom an acute persecution complex. A fairly vol-
tile combination. This time he'll be secured a
ttle more permanently. He won't bother either
ou or your father again. I'd stake my pro-
ssional reputation on it.'

The cool conviction in Jed's voice was all the
assurance she'd ever need. She sighed, tucking
er legs underneath her. Jed's measured, steady
aze was making her feel decidedly guilty. His
pecific instructions to wait for him tonight,
side the stage door, had been simple enough to
ollow. She'd nearly got them both drowned be-
ause of her pigheadedness. She could have been
tabbed tonight because of her wilful desire to
lout his authority...

'Do you still think I'm a spoiled brat?'

Jed levelled a dissecting gaze at her. She felt
er cheeks grow pink under the cool scrutiny.

'After the way you marched out of the theatre
lone tonight,' he said, 'what do you think?'

There was a long, tense silence. Ana felt her
hroat choke on a lump of angry emotion.

'Well, that's that, then,' she agreed in a small,
ollow voice. 'You've finished the job, haven't
ou? Brought the wicked criminal to justice?
aved the client from the consequences of her

own foolish actions? Send your bill to my father and find yourself another dangerous assignment to keep the adrenalin flowing...'

Jed stood up. His eyes were narrowed with a hard brilliance as he gazed down at her.

'It's not quite that simple.'

'Why?' Her heart was pumping painfully as she picked up the rougher note in his voice.

'Because meeting you has messed up my flow of adrenalin.'

'That's right, blame me for everything!' she flashed back, then stopped, frowning at him in confusion. 'What did you say? What are you talking about?'

'I'm talking about meeting you, four years ago,' he explained, raking a hand through his hair in an exhausted gesture, 'and how it affected my life...'

She regarded him wide-eyed, breathless with tension and mounting, angry disbelief.

'Are you trying to tell me that being foul tempered and cruel to me that weekend four years ago somehow affected your *life*?'

'That's not exactly the way I'd have phrased it.' The glint of rueful humour was brief. Jed's eyes were dark with an emotion she couldn't read but which seemed to be doing unspeakable things to her insides. 'I was busy being a loner, submerging my identity in strings of dangerous jobs. Somehow when I left Farthingley that weekend I found I had a different slant on things...'

'So how have you changed?'

'I've eased off. Become less...obsessional. I
un my own company. Let my employees take
he risks. I've acquired a taste for a quieter life.

don't take on bodyguard assignments any
onger,' Jed told her slowly.

She stared at him incredulously.

'Then what about me?'

His eyes moved over her flushed, tense face,
hen down to the jerky rise and fall of her breasts
inder the raspberry-pink jumper, lifting back to
neet her disbelieving brown gaze.

'You were a one-off.'

'As a favour to my father?' Her voice was
usky, a shaky whisper. Something in Jed's quiet
ntensity was destroying her composure. The
earning ache inside her was growing to a painful,
iery hunger, but she was afraid to let it, afraid
o admit it...

'No. Because I couldn't risk someone else pro-
ecting you...'

'You're not making sense.'

'If you were in danger,' he explained, with slow
recision of the kind used to children, 'it had to
e *me* protecting you, Ana. If you love someone,
ou want to protect them...'

'If you love someone...?' The heat surged and
eceded in her face, and she balled her fingers
nto tight fists to stop herself from flinging her
irms round his neck. 'Jed, if you've got some-
hing to say to me, why can't you just come right
ut and *say* it? Instead of—of pussyfooting
round like—like some fusty old solicitor,

wrapping up your meaning in a load of evasive waffle and...'

Her outburst trailed off as he gave an abrupt hoarse laugh, reached forward and cupped her hot face in his hands. Green-grey eyes locked with stormy brown ones, and then he slowly pulled her towards him.

'OK. I love you. Is that better?'

She couldn't breathe. Fighting for air, in a room which suddenly appeared to be sucked free of oxygen, she said huskily, 'Much better...'

'Ana...' he breathed her name on a shudder of need '...if I hadn't fished you out of the river I'd have drowned myself...'

'Oh, Jed...' This sweet fire was unbearable, she thought dizzily, the joy fizzing up like champagne bubbles in her heart. 'Darling Jed...'

He bent to slide one arm beneath her knees and one round her waist, then picked her up, holding her tightly to his chest. Weak with emotion, she let her forehead drop to his shoulder, linked her arms round his neck, and shivered with elation as he carried her over to the big, shadowy four-poster bed.

'I'm a masochist—I must be,' he groaned raggedly, laying her down on the cream and crimson bedspread and bending to let his head rest just above hers, searching her eyes with a haunted look. 'How the hell I imagined I could keep away from you after that night on the beach God only knows...'

'I thought you didn't enjoy it...that I did something wrong...'

'No. You didn't do anything wrong, Ana...' There was pain in his voice, as well as humour.

'You'd just broken your stupid rules?' she whispered teasingly.

'Exactly...'

'Ellen saved the situation for you yesterday at Farthingley,' she reminded him with a choked laugh, 'but I suppose you blame me for that too? For luring you into breaking your rules again?'

'No...' He reached his hands up to stroke the strands of hair back from her face, tracing his thumbs over her cheekbones, then stroking the pads of his thumbs over the full curve of her mouth. Her lips parted under the soft pressure, and she turned her head quickly and caught his thumb in her small white teeth, nipping hungrily, trembling with emotion at the heat of him so close to her.

'No?' It was a soft, provocative prompt.

'How could I blame you for anything?' he reasoned unevenly. 'And how in the name of God did I deserve two chances with your virginity, Ana, sweetheart?'

'You didn't deserve either.' She softened the words with a smile. 'You were rude and horrible to me four years ago, but it didn't seem to make any difference. I hate to boost your inflated ego even more, but you were the first man—the only man—who'd made me feel...'

'Randy?' he supplied drily.

'Sexually aroused,' she corrected him, with a breathless laugh.

'And since then?' Jed's low question held a degree of wonder and disbelief as he searched her flushed face. 'No one else aroused you? Not even a little?'

'Not enough. I couldn't forget you. And also...well, being rejected like that was pretty devastating...'

Jed closed his eyes in silent remorse.

'Ana, sweetheart, can you forgive me?'

'I can now...'

'I've loved you since I first met you in tha herb garden at Farthingley. And since then I've broken every self-imposed rule in my obsessive little book,' he breathed huskily, opening his eyes to focus on her mouth. 'You were the only female I'd allowed to provoke me. All my relationships had been on *my* terms. I'd been in control. Then I saw you. I wanted you like I'd never wanted anyone before. But I couldn't let desire cloud my concentration on protecting your father. shouldn't have let it cloud the issue with you, thi time. But I couldn't stop myself...'

'Oh, Jed...' Her nerve-ends were tingling with pleasure from her head to her toes. 'Darling Jed...'

'You held all the power,' he told her huskily 'That's what terrified me about you, right from the start. That was why I didn't come to find you when my assignment with William was over. couldn't risk it. I couldn't handle the thought o seeking you out, starting up a relationship, discovering you had far more control than I had— am I making any sense?'

'I think so,' she said carefully, feeling almost drugged with happiness. 'You wanted to...to stay whole, protect yourself from...from loving someone too much. In case you ended up hurting like you did when you lost your mother...'

'Maybe. All I know is with you I lose control, Ana, and it frightens the hell out of me...'

'Why?' she whispered, reaching to touch his hair, stroke his hard jaw, slip her fingers urgently over the width of his shoulders beneath the grey silk shirt. 'Why does it frighten you?'

'Because someone else gets the power,' he said softly, bending to touch his tongue to the parted O of her lips, then withdrawing it so that she was tantalised into wriggling beneath him. 'The power to hurt...'

'You can't love without risking being hurt...'

'I know. I know. I love you, Ana, sweetheart...'

'I love you too...and I'll never hurt you, Jed...'

'Then you'll marry me.' It was a harsh command, not a request.

'I'll marry you,' she assured him chokingly, her eyes bright as stars. 'I want you, I need you so much, I'll give up everything for you...'

'No!' His eyes darkened as he met her fierce intensity. 'No, not that. I saw you light up that stage tonight, Ana. Never give up your acting. Not for me, not for anyone else...'

The surge of love inside her seemed to expand until she thought she might burst. She pulled his head down and kissed him, hard, on the mouth.

'What if I were pregnant?' she whispered impulsively.

He jerked his head back, his eyes narrowed in smoky amusement.

'Are you telling me that you are?' There was such abrupt, husky pleasure in his voice that she bit her lip in sudden regret. 'It's far too soon to tell, sweetheart...'

'I know,' she amended ruefully, writhing as he tightened his hold on her warningly. 'But I could be, couldn't I? The thought has occurred to me once or twice. I mean, I wasn't...protected that night. And you didn't—you weren't either.'

'Another rule broken,' he agreed ruefully on a hoarse laugh. 'For the first time in my life. Well, rest assured, my darling, I'm in no hurry, but the thought of becoming a family man, with you as my wife, is just about the best prospect I've had in a long, long while...'

'If...if I was pregnant now, it wouldn't be too big a problem. There's only just over three months left of my contract with the RSC.' She blushed at the look in his eyes, and finished up unsteadily, 'I'm only trying to be practical...'

'You're very lovable when you're trying to be practical,' he assured her, with a breathtaking glitter in his eyes, 'and, since I'm no better pre-

ared tonight than I was that other night, there's
a chance your wish may come true, sweetheart...'

'Why, what did you have in mind for tonight?'
he teased recklessly, stroking the powerful slope
of his shoulders with fingers that tingled with
joyful excitement.

'You want me to spell it out?' He dropped his
head to sink his tongue between her lips, plun-
dering deep inside her mouth with explicit dem-
onstration, and she trembled convulsively as he
stretched out lazily beside her, and pulled her over
to straddle him. 'Or to put it in the vernacular,
Miss French...'

His laughing murmur was lamentably explicit,
but the caressing hands were warmly loving, and
his fierce shudder as he ground her down against
his male hardness transmitted the pent-up ferocity of his feelings.

The rest of the town slumbered through the
early hours, and the dangerous river flowed
silently through the night below their hotel
window, but, safe in the firelit shadows of the
bedroom, Ana gave a choked moan of pleasure
and surrendered herself to the blissful, ecstatic
prospect of loving Jed Steele, single-mindedly,
with all her heart, every waking minute of the
rest of her life...

This March, Harlequin brings you
a wonderful collection of
stories celebrating family, in...

YOURS, MINE
& Ours

Written by three of your favorite authors

PENNY JORDAN
CATHY GILLEN THACKER
MARISA CARROLL

How do two families become one? Just add love!
Available anywhere Harlequin books are sold.

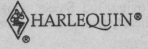

HARLEQUIN®

Look us up on-line at: http://www.romance.net

HREQ397

HARLEQUIN PRESENTS®

She couldn't let him touch her!

Coming next month:

#1873 A DAUGHTER'S DILEMMA
by
Miranda Lee

Vaughan Slater wanted Caroline more than any
woman he'd ever known. So did that mean he would
seduce her, make love to her and then walk away?
Like Carolyn knew he had, ten years before?

Available in April wherever
Harlequin books are sold.